Hollywood show runner Evans McCoy's hit TV show has just been yanked off the air thanks to its star Nora North's spectacular drug bust. Desperate to find work to qualify for Writer's Guild health insurance, Evans finds every door closed due to the problems associated with his show. His recent fling with mysterious and sexy Spanish businessman Mio-Alejo Cortez is heating up, however, and it's hard to resist the lure of Mio's invitation to visit him in Barcelona.

The city's most romantic holiday, Dia de Sant Jordi—St. George's Day—is approaching. Mio wants Evans there for the big day when lovers traditionally exchange a book and a rose. With the memory of their scorching rendezvous and constant hot faxes from Mio teasing him, Evans is unable to turn down the invitation and lands in Barcelona, full of expectations.

Evans soon learns that Mio is a man of many, many secrets and a dangerous double life. Barcelona and Mio are seductive conquerors, but when Mio's truth emerges, Evans must decide—should he cut bait and run? With his career seemingly in tatters and Mio's secret now his to share, Evans takes a gamble. He plunges headfirst into Mio's world of high-class, high-stakes sex.

The Book and the Rose
Copyright © 2019 A. J. Llewellyn
ISBN: 978-1-4874-2527-2
Cover art by Martine Jardin

Published by eXtasy Books Inc or
Devine Destinies, an imprint of eXtasy Books Inc

Look for us online at:
www.eXtasybooks.com or www.devinedestinies.com

THE BOOK AND THE ROSE

BY

A. J. LLEWELLYN

DEDICATION

To Jason and Marisa who told me about their first Dia de Sant Jordi and allowed their story to inspire this one.

CHAPTER ONE

"Mr. McCoy?"

"Hmph?" Evans McCoy came back to earth from his wonderful daydream with a sickening thud. He'd been enjoying his little mind romp . . . *back in that hotel room . . . damn . . . focus, McCoy, focus.*

Silvia, Mitch Radford's assistant, smiled down at him. "Mitch is ready to see you now."

"Thank you."

He ignored the three other men sitting in the waiting room of Heliconia Films. He'd recognized them as screenwriters as soon as they walked in. They all wore the same uniform. Low-rise jeans, loose, V-neck T-shirt, messenger bag, designer sneakers. They all wore the same confident look that masked sheer and utter desperation.

Not Evans McCoy. He'd risen the ranks from writer to producer to showrunner. He'd had the number one show on NBC for two seasons. True, the stress was sending him headfirst into an early grave, but . . . *we were number one!*

He adjusted his tie, tugged at his shirt sleeves, rebuttoned his suit jacket. His assistant Michael, a true fashionista, had overhauled his wardrobe for his job search.

Michael had insisted on good quality shirts that required cuff links. His new Boss suit weighed heavily on his credit card limit, but it helped to bolster his ego.

Silvia pushed open the door to her boss's office.

She smiled at Evans encouragingly. He'd met her once before, but they had spoken many times. This was his third attempt at a meeting with Mitch Radford. The first time Radford stood him up, leaving him languishing in the waiting room. The second time he canceled as Evans was driving onto the Warner Brothers lot.

Bad form to be sure, but Evans needed a job now. It had stunned him how hard it was to land another gig when he'd been number one just two short months ago.

It was almost a shock to see Mitch in person. Even more of a shock that he looked like a pre-teen. How old was this guy?

Evans tried to swallow his anger. Radford had made him wait for over half an hour, and he suspected the Kush ball on his desk and basketball hoop mounted on the wall had something to do with it.

They shook hands. Mitch indicated the chair opposite his, across a desk immaculate save for a movie clapper board, the Kush ball, and a toy dinosaur Evans recognized as a merchandised toy from the company's recent and catastrophic commercial flop.

"Glad you could finally make it," Mitch said, steepling his fingers together and throwing himself into his chair.

Evans stared at him for a moment. *I wasn't the one who flaked on our meetings.* He said nothing, however. He kept smiling, thinking of his Screen Writers Guild health insurance benefits. Evans needed twenty more hours of work this quarter before he could qualify for full coverage.

Damn that Nora North. She just couldn't keep her big nose away from the coke spoon.

Mitch stared at him, and he felt guilty. Had the guy said something he missed?

"They told me you were good-looking," Mitch said, "but until I saw your photo on Facebook, I had no idea. You still haven't befriended me, by the way."

Is he kidding me? Is he hitting on me?

"I'll rectify that as soon as I leave your office." Evans

knew how to turn on the charm and made Mitch laugh.

"So . . . Evans . . . is it okay if I call you Evans?"

It's my name, dumbass. "Sure."

"I know you had a really great run and some hot numbers with *Out of Step.*" He took a deep breath.

Oh, here we go.

"So tell me, how is Nora doing? Is it true she's in a lockdown facility?"

In the four weeks since he'd been actively hunting for a new job, Evans had been able to sift interviewers into two categories. Those genuinely interested in maybe giving him work, and those who wanted fresh Nora North gossip.

"She's in rehab and doing great, but as I am sure you're aware, her health comes first, and the network decided to pull the plug on the show. After all, she is . . . *was* the show."

Mitch swung in his chair. "Right, right. So tell me, is there any truth to the rumor that she took off her clothes and went running through the Paramount lot begging strange guys to fuck her?"

Shit! How much does he know? She even begged me and I'm gay!

"No. Absolutely not."

Mitch kept asking questions. Evans moved Mitch into Category B, bit down on his disappointment and bantered, feigning interest, allowing his mind to wander. He could drift and dream . . . alone on his own mental private island with Mio-Alejo Cortez, the hot Spanish businessman he'd had not just one, but two scorching encounters with. Just the thought of that man's sensuous mouth on his body made him squirm in his seat.

God, I want to call him, but I have to play it cool.

Evans still couldn't believe his luck meeting Mio on that brief trip to London. He'd never seen a man who oozed so much sex appeal. His dark, silky hair had been cropped short, but still managed to look dreamy with his widow's peak and thick, dark brows. He didn't smile much, but when he did, he was electrifying. His English had been limited when they met in the bar at the Dorchester. The second time he'd run into Mio, the man had whipped out a Spanish-English dictionary.

He'd smooth out a piece of paper on which he'd written, *I crave to speak to you*. That paper was still in his wallet. It carried Evans through some tough times dealing with his bleak moments in the Hollywood minefield.

"You are more than handsome," Mio had said. "You are beautiful."

They'd spent the afternoon and evening in bed. *Lips, eyes, mouth, tongue, teeth . . . there wasn't a part of him I didn't like . . . or spend hours lingering over.*

A late supper and a night of unhurried, but passionate, nonstop sex had ruined Evans for any of the studio idiots he met back in Los Angeles.

"You know, I met her once at a party up on Summit," Mitch was saying when Evans tuned back to the present.

Evans knew where this conversation was heading and didn't want to take this road at all. Just saying *Summit* was an industry catchword. It meant that Mitch partied—hard— and wanted to know if Evans did. Or if Evans knew about those big pool-and-sex parties up on luxurious but decadent Summit Drive.

"I know nothing about her . . . partying," Evans said. "Look, she's a friend. A friend I care deeply about. I wish her the best. I'm sure you do, too."

She fucking killed my career and my show. A show that took me six years to get into production. Right now, I fucking hate her.

"Right, right. You're right." Mitch pointed a finger at him. "She was hittin' the snort pretty hard though and . . ."

He allowed Mitch to ramble on. Evans wanted to think about Mio. Mio, who'd called him from Spain three weeks ago saying he had a business trip to Miami.

"Meet me," he'd implored. "My hands . . . they need to touch you. My mind . . . it needs you. You are my *tesoro*."

His treasure? Evans would have flown anywhere, on his own dime to see him, but having another man value him enough to fly him out first-class for a hot weekend had been alluring. They'd met at the airport . . . oh, what pleasure it had been to see Mio in his trademark Saville Row suit and hand-sewn Turnbull and Asser shirt.

Their chemistry had been undeniable . . . even more intense. They both knew their first fling had been no fluke.

He hadn't bothered Mio with much of the drama of getting Nora into lockdown, the surgery she required after destroying her septum, the cartilage between her nostrils, due to snorting so much coke. Losing the show. He'd been so delighted with the respite, the adoring attention of his handsome, debonair lover. He smiled, thinking of Mio's childlike glee in buying Chicken McNuggets, dipping them in honey and feeding them in bed to Evans . . .

Now he'd been back two weeks and two days. Each day without Mio got worse. They talked at least once a day and the calls became shorter and shorter. It hurt them both to talk . . . and also, not to talk. Evans felt tears pricking the back of his eyes. Mio had been a beautiful dream that both harmed and helped him. In some moments, he could imagine a future with him. In other moments, the slender, invisible thread between them seemed to snap.

"So what are you working on now?" Mitch asked.

Evans jerked back to reality. "I've been wanting to meet with you about doing a new series with Heliconia."

"Right, right . . ."

It galled that *Out of Step* had been his entire creation and now it was locked in contract hell with the network. He couldn't use the name or recast the lead. He had to start again.

"The thing of it is that we're not looking to get involved in television right now."

Evans remembered that last afternoon with Mio. They'd gone for a swim at the hotel pool. Mio had run into a couple of guys he knew and introduced them to Evans. They'd been such good-looking men, but before the conversation could start, Mio whisked Evans back to their room.

He was amazing. Tender... passionate... funny. I'll never meet anyone like him ever again. But our lives are separate. Ha. You might even say out of step. I need to be here, and he's as European as olive oil.

Evans smiled at Mitch. "You approached me about your new vampire series. We were supposed to—"

"Vampires are passé now, Evans. Fantastic name by the way. It's your mom's last name, right?"

"Yes."

Why did you bring me here if vampires are on the slide?

He contemplated asking the question out loud. He had nothing to lose except his health benefits, but Mitch answered it for him.

"Zombies are where it's at. Zombies are the new vampires."

"Absolutely," Evans said. "Which is what I wanted to talk to you about."

I can switch my pitch to zombies... but I thought they were hot two years ago.

"We already have two zombie shows slated. Two movies... if they fly, I'd like to talk to you about running a series for us."

Fuck! That could take another year...

"In the meantime, I was wondering... I don't have a job I can give you, but I thought... you know... maybe we could have dinner one night... soon?"

Mio's body... hard, smooth, skin the color of caramel... yet he couldn't keep his mouth off mine.

"No," he said. "I'm involved."

"Oh . . ." That threw Mitch. He was used to being the guy in charge, clearly. "That's weird . . . only I asked around, and word on the vine is that you're single."

"I don't . . ." Evans took a breath. "I'm pretty private, Mitch." He stood. "Thanks for the meeting. I really appreciate your time."

Mitch scrambled out of his chair. "Oh . . . well, thank you. Uh . . . have a nice day."

Evans shook his hand and looked him in the eye. "You have a nice day, too, Mitch." *You jerk.*

He walked out of the office, past Silvia's desk. She didn't glance up at him, and he knew she'd listened to the whole thing. She didn't look up because the business meeting had gone badly and her boss's clumsy attempt at getting a date had flopped.

This was the latest in technological progress. Studio executives bugged their offices during meetings so that pesky writers couldn't claim they'd stolen ideas after pitch meetings, which they routinely did.

"Thank you, Silvia," he said, mindful of being polite and friendly with her. Today's personal assistant could be tomorrow's studio boss.

She glanced up, smiled and also wished him a nice day.

Yeah, nice. He stood outside and checked his cell phone for messages. He longed for a call, just one little text from Mio. He remembered their last moments, Mio between his legs, fucking him, his mouth clamped over Evans'.

I never wanted to leave him.

He called his agent, Kelly King, who took his call immediately.

"How did it go?"

"A bust. He wanted a date."

"I hope you said yes."

He laughed.

7

"Are you going over to visit Nora?" she asked.

"Yeah."

"Well, you'll need a drink after that. It's on me. I'll meet you over at Residuals. Let's say one?"

"Are you kidding me? I don't start that early."

"Oh, excuse me." He loved Kelly. She always made him laugh. "How's five o'clock?"

"Sounds good to me."

He ended the call, got into his six-month-old Prius and thought about calling his assistant, Michael, who was hanging by a thread emotionally and financially. Evans helped the guy out with bills and with constant pep talks. When the show was canceled, he'd promised Michael he'd find them a job, he'd take him with him. Nora North's drug addiction had not just wrecked his show, she'd demolished the hopes of the wonderful crew Evans had fought hard to assemble.

Now it looked like she had ruined his career. He was being punished for her sins in Hollywood.

I'm all washed up, and I'm only thirty-two.

Evans pushed out of the parking lot and hit a red light. It was a long one. He sat, not wanting to listen to music or talk radio. All he wanted was Mio's smile. To hear his laugh one more time. The sun sparkled, and it should have heartened him after long weeks of unprecedented rain. Except that high above him overlooking Riverside Drive, the poster of perky, pretty Nora North promoting *Out of Step,* a poster that had been there for months was being covered up.

He watched the workmen with long-handled sticks pasting up the long, single sheets that would make one gigantic poster.

A part of him wanted to step on the gas and go straight out into the intersection and let the other, unsuspecting drivers kill him. A part of him wanted to . . . no, *needed* to stay alive in case Mio called.

His cell phone rang, and he plugged it into his dashboard

circuit.

"Hello," he said.

"*Hola*, Evans."

The light turned green, and a car honked him from behind.

It was him. It was Mio.

CHAPTER TWO

The next sound Evans heard was the squall of brakes from the guy behind him trying not to plough straight into his Prius. The guy leaned on the horn and Evans shot forward.

"What's going on?" Mio asked.

"I almost got in an accident."

"That's not good."

"No, not good. See what you do to me? I hear your voice, and I drive like an idiot."

"Ah, then it is good." The sultry chuckle coming over his radio almost sent him driving on the sidewalk.

"I'm pulling over so I can talk to you."

"You have hands-free cell phone, no?"

"Yeah, but I want to talk to you, Mio."

There was a pause. Then, "*Te extrano*, Evans."

"God, I miss you, too."

"How was it today?"

Evans smiled in spite of his anxiety. He wouldn't have told Mio anything except that Mio had Skyped him at four o'clock in the morning and Evans had blurted the news of a big interview. Evans was so addicted to his lover he slept with his laptop turned on beside him so they could have continuous access to one another. "The best part of my day is this phone call."

"*Me vuelves loco*," Mio said, his voice a low grunt.

"Good." Evans laughed for the first time that day. "You drive me crazy, too."

He heard voices on Mio's side of the conversation.

"I crave to speak to you."

Mio knew this single sentence could get Evans flat on his back in no time. "But I have to go . . . I call you back, *guapo*."

"Okay," Evans said. God, it was like trying to hold onto a dragonfly.

He was used to these calls, with hot-nothings exchanged, the pauses with so much *not* being said. Sometimes Mio needed to go. He was a busy guy with his furniture import-export business. When Evans was working, he was exactly the same. Some small crisis would crop up. It took another busy man to understand it wasn't rudeness to hang up. It was business.

Evans didn't know much about Mio's work and Mio didn't discuss it unless Evans pushed. Mio was more interested in Evans' work. He had never seen a single episode of *Out of Step*, which made it so much easier for Evans to confess his frustration over the cancelation of the show when Mio pushed finally for details.

Mio was the only guy he knew who didn't want Nora North gossip, yet oddly, he was the only one who knew just how sick the actress really was.

And Mio had called him *guapo*, gorgeous. *Man, I'm like a teenager with this guy.*

Evans headed east to the Behavioral Health Center at Alhambra Hospital. He checked the time. He had twenty minutes. He was halfway there when Mio called back.

"Guapo?"

Evans laughed. "You're the guapo, baby."

"No, you."

They both laughed.

"You are good for me," Mio said, his voice like hot tea steeped in orange mint and honey. It soothed Evans' soul.

Before Evans could respond, Mio's words came out in a rush.

"I have to see you, Evans. To touch you. I want you to

11

come and visit me."

Evans found himself smiling. "Where?"

"Here, in Barcelona."

Thank God he was driving because Evans would otherwise have been in serious danger of doing the Snoopy Dance.

"I'd love that."

"*Tsk*. I call you back. Where are you?"

"In my car."

"You live in your car? You are always in it."

"Some days it feels like that."

"Where you going?"

"To the hospital."

"To visit . . . *her*?"

Mio always said *her*, in a tone suggesting she was Hitler, which wasn't far from the truth.

"*Sí*."

"Why?" Mio sounded distressed. "Will you be alone?"

"The doctor will be there."

Mio sighed. "You are a good man, Evans. Too good."

"Thank you, Mio."

"I call you tonight. Now I have two meetings. And I will have to worry about you. *Ciao ciao*."

God, even the way he says goodbye is sexy. I think I am falling hard for this guy.

He drove in a blissful cloud of memories, veering off the Rosemead Boulevard exit on the freeway just in time. The hospital loomed ahead on his right, and he felt the familiar discomfort he experienced the night he and Michael had brought Nora here after a frightening episode when she tried to kill herself.

Evans parked his car, pocketing his cell phone. He had been here once to visit Nora since the horrifying night when he had staged an intervention and found her in her Echo Park apartment with self-inflicted knife wounds on her legs

12

and arms. She'd stabbed herself in the hands and feet and insisted they were stigmata.

At the front desk, he was subjected to his ID being scrutinized, and the nurse walked in as he was signing his name.

"Mr. McCoy, I'm so pleased to see you. I think Hamish is expecting you, isn't he?"

"Yes, he is."

Hamish was the psychiatrist who'd been on hand when the ambulance brought Nora here. She'd come in like a screaming B-movie queen in a straight jacket, out of control and out of her mind. It still upset him to think about it. She'd been sedated and examined. They transferred her to the main hospital opposite the mental health clinic for surgery on her nose and stitches to her deeper wounds. Hamish had remained in steady contact with Evans ever since, as the outside point person for Nora's recovery.

The nurse reached for a file, consulted it and said, "Please take a seat. We'll be right with you."

Hamish, a very good-looking blond man on loan from a Bangor, Maine hospital, came to the double set of glass doors within seconds. Evans stood as Hamish clasped his hand with both of his. They greeted one another warmly. Hamish had recognized a caring soul in Evans, a different sort of Hollywood TV producer. Evans had recognized in Hamish a strong man who could stand up to the wackiest chick to ever bounce into his asylum.

They walked through the first door, and it closed right behind them so fast even a housefly couldn't have squeezed through it before the second door became activated.

Evans was here as a visitor, not a patient, but he still felt a ridiculous pang of terror at the idea of being locked in here, of not being allowed to leave.

Hamish took Evans through two more sets of security doors before leading him into his office. It was a light-filled room with happy plants and colorful books on shelves. He recognized standard self-help titles like *You Can Heal Your Life* and *The Gifts of Imperfection* stacked against weightier texts.

He sat across from the doctor, who came straight to the point.

"She's a nightmare."

"Yeah," Evans said. "I know."

"I have a problem. She won't take her meds, so her delusions are worse than ever. I put her in the actors' ward — "

"There's an actors' ward?"

Hamish nodded. "And a writers' ward."

Evans ran a hand over his face. *What about a showrunners' ward? I bet there's a waiting list for that one.*

"She refuses the meds, and she is very loud . . . and so our other patients are not only dealing with their psychoses but hers as well."

"Oh, my God."

"She's convinced the others that the food and even the water here are poisoned. I won't be able to keep her here if she doesn't cooperate. But I'm worried. She's legally insane, and she's been certified, but unless she starts complying, I won't be able to keep her here."

Evans absorbed the news. "What do you want me to do?"

"I need you to talk to her, convince her she needs the pills."

"I can try. Is she . . . is she . . . still violent?"

"No. Now that she's off the cocaine and crystal meth, the physical episodes no longer occur. Your eye looks much better, by the way."

"Thanks."

It was amazing how good Michael could be with makeup. Though the eye was better, a sallow color still lurked under it and on top of his left cheekbone.

Mio had gone crazy when Evans had showed up in Miami with a black eye. He'd spotted it in spite of makeup. He'd gone even crazier when Evans told him the story of how he'd had to fight to get Nora off him in his first visit. No matter what recovery she made, he knew Mio would never forgive Nora—or even like her.

"You're a good man," Hamish said.

"So everybody keeps telling me." Evans leaned forward. "Look, she doesn't have anyone else."

Hamish grew quiet. "She has her Twitter fans. She told me this morning it's all she cares about. Tweeting. She's become obsessed with cell phones. She hasn't been able to tweet for weeks, and she's becoming belligerent about it." He paused. "She's the worst patient I've ever had."

He read from some notes in front of him. "She's allowed to make calls from the pay phone when she behaves. The only people she has called are you, the head of NBC, and a dead phone number. She calls this one obsessively."

Hamish pushed a piece of paper toward him. "Do you recognize it?"

Evans studied it for several seconds. It was familiar. He took his cell phone out and rifled through his stored numbers.

"It's the phone number to our stage manager's on-set office." Evans took a deep breath. "He was the guy she always had to call to check in with. You see . . . we hired two assistants to watch her in our last weeks of production. She had a tendency to escape. Our show was a sitcom with a very light, but rigid schedule. We had a read-through of the script every Tuesday, rehearsed Wednesday, shot location scenes on Thursday, if there were any, and filmed the actual episode live on Friday afternoons in front of an audience. She never showed up to read-throughs or rehearsals in the end . . . and she had to call Curly—"

"Curly?"

"The stage manager. She was given a lot of leeway as long a she called Curly and let him know she'd be there Friday. She has . . . had . . . an uncanny gift of photographic memory. She could look at a page of script and remember it verbatim. She was a total pro on Fridays. She was just a bitch on wheels the rest of the time . . . and then she started to fall apart on Fridays. Before that, we thought we could cope."

Hamish stared at him. "Are they . . . are they all like this?"

Evans shrugged. "Actresses? She's not unusual in terms of being an addict, but studios are less inclined to put up with the nonsense now because of insurance. Nobody would insure the show once she got arrested for running down Ventura Boulevard naked . . . it went downhill from there."

Hamish held up the piece of paper. "Why is Curly's number disconnected?"

Evans shrugged. "It's one of hundreds the studio has. It will be reactivated I'm sure for the next production . . . it's recycled constantly." He looked at Hamish. "And you say she keeps calling this number?"

"All day long."

"She's . . . it's like she thinks this is all a big TV show and she's . . . she's giving a performance."

Hamish nodded. "Listening to what you're telling me, it makes sense. I agree with your assessment. She thinks she's Norma Desmond and she's in her own version of *Sunset Boulevard*. Look, she's requested that you see her. Demanded it actually. She's had a few people who call and ask about her, mostly the tabloids, pretending to be family members."

"I know, and I'm grateful that you've protected her privacy so well. Hamish, I'm worried that if she gets out, she'll go straight back to using. She needs this place."

"We're in full agreement there. She does very well one-on-one, which is typical I think, for some artistic types. She's frankly a pain in the ass in group therapy because she takes over. She makes up stories, she rants, and she says mean things to the other patients. Unfortunately, our treatment here revolves around group therapy."

"What are you recommending? I mean, this isn't my field of expertise. I'm just the guy who stopped her from killing herself." Evans swallowed, trying not to think about he and Michael had found her, awash in blood, ranting incoherently. He had staunched the blood with his own hands and had cleaned her home himself so the tabloids wouldn't find out about it.

Hamish lifted his hands. "I'm not giving up on her. I frankly think she would do well on medication. I've tried negotiating with her. I've offered to release her on the proviso she gets daily counseling, and she's taking meds. She seems to get it, then she flies off the handle."

"I know. I asked people who knew her before she got heavily into drugs and they say she was always difficult, but never . . . nasty. I worked with her on a movie, and she was your normal, garden-variety, highly-strung diva. I could handle her. Now . . . I don't know who she is and she terrifies me."

"Understandably. I think she's finally realizing she's very lucky that she has you in her corner. She was very resentful of you for bringing her here. She's since seen a photograph of herself from that night. She realizes you saved her life."

Evans nodded. *She still scares the crap out of me.* "She has nobody else, Hamish. I want to help."

Hamish looked at him for a long moment. "When you were here last, she had bandages on her nose. She requires another surgery. I'm telling this so you won't be shocked. Her nose is missing the septum. This has been devastating for her, but until she's well enough, her heartbeat back to normal, the surgeons at the main hospital don't want to risk a second surgery."

Oh, God. She's the vainest woman in America. She must be

17

flipped out over this.

"I'll take you out to her. She's sitting at the rec table. Just so you know, she's argumentative but . . ." He smiled. "I think you're used to that by now."

He followed Hamish outside. The sun shone, delicious and warm, casting a glorious halo effect around the plants and trees in the courtyard. A pair of pigeons sat in a tree. It was a cozy image, with a few people sitting at tables reading, chatting. One man sat with his face in the sun.

Nora sat at a wooden table, all alone, huddled around a mound of torn pages from a magazine. She kept ripping pages as she eyed Evans walking toward her.

"How are you doing?" He squeezed her shoulder. She shrugged him off.

"I'm doing lousy. Think of all the money I'm losing being in here. I can't even order any of these clothes online." She pulled a face like a little kid and tore out another page. Her anger was always daunting, always . . . unfathomable.

"Evans came to visit you," Hamish said.

"I can see that." She twisted her face again. Boy, she was in a mood all right.

Hamish had warned him about her nose, but it was still disturbing to see a nose with no cartilage. It was flat and weird-looking. He tried not to stare at it. He wondered if she was in pain.

"They poisoned my food last night," Nora said. "And they say they don't, but I know." She held a page between her thin hands. "Did you know they have spies all over the building?"

"No, they don't." Evans could feel another barn-burner of a headache building behind his eyes.

"Yes, they do. And I know you know all about it, you *fucking Nazi.*"

She screamed so loud, the pigeons flew off their branch, scattering to the ledge of the roof.

Nora's eyes glinted with mischief . . . and madness.

"I'm Jewish," Evans said.

"You're still a Nazi, you fucking homo." There was such violence in her tone, he inched his chair back.

"No, I'm not. I'm your brother, remember?"

"My parents didn't want you. They gave you up for adoption, remember?"

"Yes, I remember." *You are such a bitch. I think actually prefer you when you're stoned.*

She began shredding the pages. "You and all the other fucking Nazis can read my mind. All my thoughts are in these pages. Why won't you die?"

Evans turned and looked at Hamish whose face registered his shock and despair.

"I think I need to leave," Evans said.

"No, you need to die, Nazi."

Hamish's eyes widened as he led Evans away. "She wasn't this bad an hour ago."

"Just my lucky day, I guess."

Evans felt utter devastation. This was worse than the last meeting when she punched him in the face.

"Are you okay?" Hamish asked. "You look very pale."

"My sister hates me."

"No, she hates herself."

Why, oh why had his sister tracked him down? He'd been astonished to discover they were kin. The Nora he read about in the tabloids always seemed a kooky kinda gal. She said her life was empty, meaningless without him. Now she wanted him to die.

The TV show was supposed to be their way of being together, working with one another . . . making up for the lost years. Only a handful of people knew of the exact nature of his relationship with Nora.

She had stopped speaking to both her parents and they were not interested in meeting Evans. He didn't really care to meet them, either. He had two parents that he loved and who were devastated when Nora came into the picture.

His adopted mother panicked, thinking Evans would abandon them.

In Miami, when Mio had seen his face, Evans had told him the truth. He'd been relieved to tell somebody, to share the reality of his life with him.

"It is strange that you were the one given away, but she's the one who is so fucked up," Mio had said.

Back in his car, Evans gripped the wheel. He cried out of anguish and frustration. He felt guilty that his sister was sick. He had no idea how to help her. He felt guilty that he was happy to be away from the hospital . . . away from her. He wanted to see his parents, the only parents he knew, but they were in the Caribbean on a well-deserved vacation. He couldn't talk to them about *her.*

He blew his nose, pulled himself together and called Michael.

"Hey, you feel like some lunch?"

"I always feel like some lunch."

"Great, I'll pick you up in thirty minutes."

"How did the meeting go?"

Evans accidentally dropped the phone and quickly picked it up again. "My meeting was a washout. I thought we were discussing business, he thought we were on a date."

The line crackled. "He hit on you?"

Evans tensed. *My God, it's Mio. Please be dreaming . . . did my phone call him? Did it jog the call waiting feature?*

"Mio?"

"*Sí, señor.* Who is this guy who hits on my *novio*?"

Evans smiled. He loved their little *sí señor* jokes. He laughed. "Nobody."

"Did you tell him you have a boyfriend?"

"*Sí, señor.*"

Evans was certain he could hear Mio smiling on the other

end of the phone.

"So, now you must come to Barcelona. I need to fuck you some more . . . you're too hot over there in California."

Evans loved the way Mio pronounced California.

"I need to remind you about how we Spaniards treat our lovers. I'll arrange your trip. You come for two weeks. I need you here, *mi rey*."

"Two weeks?" Evans was aware of Michael languishing on the other end of the line.

"I have to go, Mio, I'm sorry. We'll talk about this later."

"I call you with the details. I book your trip. I need you here for La Díada de Sant Jordi."

"Díada de Sant Jordi. Day of . . . Saint . . ."

"George," Mio said.

"When is that?"

"April twenty-third."

"But Mio —"

The line went dead. Evans clicked back over to Michael. "What does *mi rey* mean?"

"My king."

Evans beamed. He cruised onto the freeway in the best mood he'd been in for two weeks and two days.

He drove home in a beautiful daze and pulled into the driveway of his Studio City house on Sunshine Terrace. It wasn't a big house. It was a cabin-style cottage south of Ventura Boulevard, high on a hill. He loved everything about his home, even the long stairs up to it. He loved his view of the main drag from the north, the Hollywood Hills from the east and the bizarre but always interesting pirate's galleon that was his neighbor's house glimpsed from his kitchen window.

The only thing he didn't like was the gigantic window facing the street that for some reason attracted every bird in the world. On beautiful days, and there were many of those in Los Angeles, they smashed into it, falling to his sun deck, dazed. So far none had died, but it always upset him.

Michael was out back in the guesthouse, which Evans had converted to two offices. There wasn't much of a garden, a mere strip really, but both rooms looked out onto it, and to the small, bricked sundeck Evans had built with his father. The view of downtown Studio City's tiny, narrow and hilly streets made him think of France or Germany. Michael waved to him from his desk in his office. He was on the phone.

Evans gave him a finger wave back and moved straight to the fax machine. Mio was an old-fashioned guy for someone who was thirty-four. He hated texting, hated email. He either talked on the phone, via Skype, or sent faxes. The faxes he sent Evans made his toes curl on impact, they were so erotic. There was a fresh one lying on top of his mail.

He was pretty certain Michael would have read it. In fact, he could tell by Michael's sudden silence that he was pissed.

I got your results, Mio wrote. *Big smile.*

Evans had one too. He and Mio had sent each other copies of their latest blood tests. They wanted to have sex without condoms. The exchange of such information *and* a negative result were like going to third base in a gay relationship. Evans swung in his chair, loosened his tie and grinned as Mio described Barcelona's beauty and the only thing missing was him.

There are roses everywhere. April is the month for lovers, guapo. You will love it here.

Evans scanned the details of his flight confirmation. All he had to do was check his emails, click Mio's frequent flyer account link, and he would be on his way to —

"What do you mean you're going to Barcelona?"

Michael stormed into his office, hands on hips, like an angry housewife. A few years before, when he'd first met Michael, he'd contemplated a relationship and gave him a job instead. Sometimes, like now, Michael overstepped his boundaries.

"Calm down," he said. "I'm just thinking about it."

"*Thinking* about it? I've cleaned my apartment six times in the last week. I've cleaned out my closets so many times I'm left with practically *nothing* to wear. I've worn out my DVD of *The Secret*. I've feng-shuied the hell out of my life, and I'm still coming up empty."

Evans rifled through his phone messages. Nothing important and no pitch meetings scheduled according to his empty month-at-a-time calendar.

"You tried ritual sacrifice, Mike?"

"No. Are you offering yourself for my salvation?"

"Not today, no."

"It's this guy. This . . . this conquistador of yours. He's got you thinking you can have a life. Don't you know you can't do that?"

"I can't?" Evans was amused now. Michael could be hilarious when he went on one of his rants. He longed to read the fax, study his lover's handwriting. Deciphering his Spanish was half the fun of his faxes, knowing that Mio took his time to send him these notes. They were the grooviest thing that ever happened to his fax machine.

"Listen, Ev." Michael wagged a finger at him. "Miami was one thing. I tolerated you indulging in two days of sexual heat . . . you know, clear out the cobwebs, get you back in the game, but I've got an Amex bill that needs to get paid."

Evans shook his head. "Let's kill ourselves then."

"Good idea. You go first."

"No, you."

They stared at each other and laughed. It released some tension.

Michael picked at the seam of his T-shirt hem. "I'm really

panicked. I know you're still paying me, but I'm freaking out here. How long can you keep doing that without having a job?"

Evans sighed. He felt a rush of fury. "Michael, I've done my best by you. I told you if I got work, I'd take you with me, but I'm not getting work. Not even close, but I'm still paying you, so please, back off, huh? "

The good vibes he'd been feeling evaporated. What the hell was he doing? Michael was right. He couldn't go to Barcelona . . . hell, not for two weeks and not *now*.

On the other hand, why not? Nothing was keeping him here. He couldn't get arrested right now, probably not even if he got caught on Hollywood Boulevard with a transvestite hooker. Two weeks in Spain with a man he genuinely liked would be amazing.

Michael raved some more, and Evans cut him off.

"Let's skip lunch. I'm gonna make more calls . . . how about if I book you for a massage?"

"Really? You know, I am *super* stressed out."

Yeah, but I'm not, I suppose. Evans dialed the number for Burke Williams on La Brea Avenue and found they'd just had a cancelation. He booked Michael for a two-hour session and instructed him to bring him back a chicken salad from Gelson's.

"Get whatever you want, too."

"Fantastic." Michael seemed excited now. "If the massage therapist wants to give me a happy ending, can I charge it to your card?"

"No, you can't. That's illegal. I hope he doesn't want to do that. And don't forget my salad."

Evans watched him leave. Michael, in spite of his meltdowns, was the best assistant he'd ever had, until the show got canceled. He now obsessed on things and moaned and groaned . . . too often. Evans picked up his fax.

He wanted so badly to spend time with Mio. It was his for the taking . . . he shut his mind to the prospect just for now and returned to the task of finding work. He called his friend Stu, who had produced his first effort as a screenwriter a few years before. Stu was location scouting in Croatia with a new sword-and-sandal series he had in mind. Evans' call went to voice mail. It was the same with everyone he called. He tried not to take it personally.

Evans was so desperate to redeem himself even the show in Croatia would be better than nothing. His agent had mentioned a new western series — or an *oater* in movie speak — to be shot in Mexico. He'd had two meetings on the series but no call back.

I feel like a friggin' actor. I really understand how they feel.

He stared at the list of names and numbers he'd jotted down to call. His desk phone rang.

"Hey Evans," said a peppy male voice.

He recognized it as Larry Jenkins, one of the executives in charge of production at the network.

"Hi, Larry." *Maybe he has a job for me!*

"We're getting some flak from Standards and Practices," Larry said.

"About what?" Standards and Practices, the network department that scrutinized all the studios' shows before they went to air were both a blessing and a curse. Many religious and conservative groups could be counted on to protest any show's content for countless reasons and networks relied on S and P to be the rabid pit bull. The department was the butt of many a stand-up comedian's jokes, but when they slammed the door on one of your episodes airing, there wasn't much to laugh about.

"Well, they claim Nora North's ad-libbed line about *bad speed* in the final episode is drug language."

"What?"

"They want to can it."

Evans digested this bit of news. The final four episodes of the show had been airing to even higher ratings and rave reviews than before, the ultimate irony when the show was canned, and its creator couldn't get work. Everyone involved with the show agreed the freak-factor of an ailing star might have drawn all those viewers, but the show had been a huge hit before Nora North's dramatic collapse.

"Larry," he said, with all the dignity he could muster, "she never ad-libbed a line that was inappropriate. What you think is *bad speed* is actually *Godspeed*. It was a very appropriate line back in the day . . . you know people would say it . . . instead of goodbye. It was a very nice thing to say . . . like good luck to you. Good fortune. In the context of telling her lover whom she's just dumped, *Godspeed*, it was pretty funny."

Better than fuck you, which I am dying to say to you right now. Geez, Nora could deliver a line . . . she could make any line seem hysterical.

He could hear Larry turning pages. "What was the original line?"

Evans checked his shooting script. "Hit the road, Jack."

"Oh, right." Larry's voice grew faint. "I see the penciled-in *Godspeed*."

Evans said nothing. Both men knew that it was Larry's idea to hire interns to retype actual shooting scripts for S and P and somebody had messed up. Evans was just glad it hadn't been somebody in his own office.

"Okay. I'll get back to you." Larry ended the call, and Evans wondered how many heads would roll over a single misspelled word.

His agent, Kelly, had already had a cocktail, maybe two, by the time Evans arrived at Residuals at five.

Typing fast texts on her cell phone in the semi-dark and grungy industry bar, she didn't see Evans approaching, but

Boone Stanley Hatch did.

One of the oldest working actors in the business, he sat on his usual stool at the bar bullying a cluster of starstruck newcomers. A real charmer when he was sober, Hatch became a nasty drunk after a lot of drinks. Typical old-timer, but the son of a gun could sure hold his liquor until that happened. By the end of the evening, he'd be in a brawl with one of his breathless sycophants.

Hatch swiveled on his stool, held up his tumbler of straight Canadian rye and saluted Evans. "Howdy, hotshot, saw your billboard get all tored up today."

His crowd of fans snickered. Hatch must have been on his way to total inebriation to be this snarky so early in the day. Hatch had forgotten that it was Evans who got him a gig on his show when he was on Station Twelve. That was industry slang for having unpaid Guild dues. Evans had given him work and ensured the old fart got paid enough to cover his union fees and to have something left over.

He ignored the old coot. The next time he called Evans with a sob story, Evans would make sure he did what everybody else in town did, let him go to voice mail.

Kelly leaned across her stool and kissed his cheek. She whispered in his ear, "Don't mind him. He just lost a part to Ian McKellen."

Evans kissed Kelly, and she stared at him.

"What's going on? You lost your mojo?"

Kelly was a thirty-something woman who represented screenwriters, producers, and showrunners like Evans. He'd made her a lot of money in the two years they'd worked together, but neither of them had seen the kinda bucks he got with *Out of Step*, the biggest deal she'd ever brokered.

It boosted her cache . . . until the north wind blew.

"Do we need to talk shop?" he asked.

She never wanted to talk shop. He knew she must have

been upset to be doing it on their social time when she knew he'd had a crappy meeting that day.

"My partners are freaking. They say clients want to leave because we . . . well . . . they kinda promised some of the actors they could be on your show." She grimaced. "And a few of the directors."

I don't need to have anyone else's worries on my shoulders. You're my agent. You're supposed to help carry the load, not pile on more stuff.

"Well, what can I say? You're gonna have to broker another big deal, baby." He tried to catch the bartender's eye. He needed a drink. He wanted a drink. He scanned the bar menu. Michael of course, had forgotten his salad.

He watched Kelly texting somebody as Hatch berated some kid beside him and pulled out his cell phone. Evans tapped into his emails, found one from Larry saying S and P was still pulling the final episode. He didn't read through the whole explanation. He could protest the decision in writing within thirty days.

How ridiculous. He felt empty, powerless . . . useless. He saw the email with the pending confirmation code for his trip to Barcelona.

Evans clicked the link. He felt a ripple of irresponsibility as well as excitement. In two days, he'd be on his way to Spain.

CHAPTER THREE

M io was the most exciting lover he'd ever had. Having made his decision to visit him, Evans felt he was in two worlds for the next two days, half of him going through the motions of everyday tasks, Michael like a pesky bug in his ear.

The other half of him was in a beautiful state of limbo imagining his arrival in Barcelona. His conversations with Mio became even briefer, with his lover saying he'd pick him up at the airport.

As he sat in his first-class seat on American Airlines, Evans sipped champagne. He never allowed himself to drink alcohol when he was flying because it dehydrated him, but Mio had insisted he have one glass, to celebrate.

He had a long flight, fifteen hours with a stopover in London, where he would change planes to an Iberia Airlines flight. Mio said he'd pick him up in a limo so they could fool around in the backseat, just as they had when he'd arrived in Miami.

I can't wait!

He closed his eyes. He should be listening to his Spanish language lessons he'd downloaded onto his iPhone. Instead, his mind replayed the scene of his last, unpleasant afternoon with Michael, who'd trailed him around Book Soup as Evans selected a few travel guides for his trip.

"You can't be serious. You can't go to Barcelona."

They'd driven to Fry's next, so Evans could pick up a new FAA-approved laptop bag for his computer, a European electrical adapter, and an extra battery.

He mentally checked off all the things he still had to do as Michael kept up his prattle in the driver's seat beside him. His thoughts had gone from the notebook in which he'd started taking notes for a new TV series, to the way Mio would lick under and around his nipple, repeatedly. Nobody had ever made love to him the way Mio did. He actually came just from Mio finally sucking on his nipple.

Michael kept up his mantra of, "You can't be serious. Jesus dude, we need a job."

Evans frowned. "Boy, are you ever raining on someone's parade."

Michael slapped the dashboard. "Well, I'm just not thinking about it. You'll come to your senses. You won't go."

But he did.

Evans accepted a refill from his sexy flight attendant and smiled to himself, thinking about the last time he'd glimpsed Mio in a tight black T-shirt with black pants and belt. He was muscular but lean. His demeanor signaled danger. You would never know he was gay, except for his tendency to touch Evans constantly.

The champagne bubbles tickled his nostrils. Evans had downloaded articles online about places of interest, especially romantic restaurants, and gay beaches. He had read his travel guides. Now he just had to get to Mio. He hoped to God there wasn't some freak on board with explosives in his underpants. After a careful look around him, he was relieved not to see anyone looking wild-eyed, and put on his earbuds.

He listened to the hypnotic, sexy voice telling him, *Dejeme solo!* Leave me alone!"

That, he thought, was apt. *Don't think about Michael. Just relax.*

He didn't hit turbulence until he arrived at Heathrow, and that was on the ground, not in midair.

Evans had worried midflight that he hadn't locked his house. He'd paid his housekeeper, Stella, to water the plants and collect his mail, but instructed her not to allow Michael in the house. The last time he'd been away, Michael house-sat for him and had a wild cocktail party that left his neighbors spitting-mad and his house smelling like patchouli oil and marijuana.

Touching down at Heathrow, he turned on his cell phone and called Stella and was dismayed when Michael answered the phone.

"What are you doing there?" he asked. Michael started to respond, and Evans got a call on the other line. Mio.

"Hola, guapo? Are you in London?"

"Sí, señor."

Mio chuckled.

"Your ass is mine. See you in a few hours." Mio blew him a noisy, wet-sounding kiss and ended the call.

By the time he clicked back over to Michael, he was in such a good mood, he was less inclined to bite his assistant's head off.

"Luke dumped me," Michael said. This was a surprise. He and his ten-year partner had always seemed like a very strong, happy couple. In spite of Michael's relentless nu-roses.

"What happened?" Evans asked eyeing the pastries at the Costa Coffee Boutique. He bought a large coffee and a newspaper, walking to his departure gate.

"Luke said he was worried about the future."

"That's ridiculous. You're earning a wage."

"I'm not on a TV show anymore."

"And that matters?"

Michael sounded forlorn. "Apparently it does to him."

"You're better off without him." Evans sipped his coffee. He wondered which century it had been brewed in and

31

dumped it out in a trash can.

"Yeah. I guess." Michael sounded so forlorn it was infuriating,

"You can stay, but you are not to have any parties. And you are not to smoke weed or anything else in my house," Evans said.

Michael made a choking, sobbing sound and ended the call.

Evans shrugged. In a few hours, he'd be with Mio. *I can't wait to say,* estoy loco por ti. *I'm crazy about you.*

Evans scanned the carnival that made up Barcelona International Airport's arrivals area. He'd gone through immigration formalities and retrieved his suitcase, winding up in the arrivals section a little after two o'clock on a sunny afternoon. The giddy vibe and the anticipation of seeing his lover again began to falter. There was no sign of Mio. Several chauffeurs held up signs with people's last names written on them. Just as he had in Miami, he hunted for *McCoy,* but none of them held up a sign with his name.

As families, lovers, and friends found one another, the crowd thinned, and he started to worry. He checked his iPhone. It was two-forty.

And then he saw his face. Mio swaggered toward him. Evans' heart flip-flopped as he watched his lover's seductive stride. His manly confidence and sexual heat drew the gazes of men and women alike. He wore jeans and an open-necked white shirt.

It was not until Evans looked down that he saw a tiny boy, no more than two-years-old, clinging to Mio's pant leg.

"*Hola,*" Mio said, gripping Evans' hand. "How was your flight?"

Who the hell is the kid? And a handshake? All I get is a handshake? I'm ready for hot sex, and he's shaking my hand?

Evans stared at the toddler as Mio swept the child into his

arms. He saw a woman over Mio's left shoulder. She was gorgeous. She had shiny, chestnut-colored hair that swung to her shoulders. She wore a pretty yellow sundress, and she held a baby in her arms.

Holy shit! He's married!

"Belen, come and meet Evans."

The little boy in Mio's arms clung to his neck. His big, brown eyes never left Evans' face.

Evans felt his body swaying a little as she stepped forward. *Who the hell is she?*

"This is my sister, Belen." Mio turned to her. "And this is my friend, Evans, from America."

Evans was surprised to see that Mio was nervous.

So was Evans. It was clear Mio's sister didn't speak English. The kids stared at him. He racked his brains for something to say other than, *estoy loco por ti.*

"Hi," he said, like an idiot.

She grinned, and he quickly added, "*No quiero vivir sin ti.*"

Holy shit! I just told her I can't live without her!

Mio threw his head back and laughed. "Is there something you haven't told me? You like women now?" He cupped the back of Evans' head with his free hand, his dazzling smile shifting to his sister. "Isn't he beautiful?"

He dropped his hand, his gaze moving to Evans' single suitcase and laptop bag.

"Is this all you brought? Are you sure you're gay?"

"Belen, I meant to say pleased to meet you," Evans said, desperate.

"Don't worry. Since you can't live without Belen, I think she knows that."

This time, Evans laughed.

"Welcome to the happiest city in the world," Mio said. "Here, guapo, you hold Primo. I'll take the bags."

Mio pushed the toddler in his arms and Evans got a whiff of figs . . . and lime. God, it was Mio's scent.

"I'm pleased to meet you, too, Evans." Belen's English was pretty good. Like Mio's, it was heavily-accented. She jiggled the baby in her arms. "And this is Violeta."

Primo started to fidget and whine in Evans' arms as they left the terminal.

Oh great, just my luck his nephew hates me!

Primo's little arms shot out to Mio, who was busy hustling toward a gleaming silver Renault convertible. A policeman, ticket book in hand, walked toward the vehicle. He stopped and shook his head when he saw Mio's family had already reached the vehicle.

He shook a finger at Mio, who laughed.

Two baby seats in the back of the car surprised Evans. He couldn't imagine anyone in L.A. driving a convertible with the top down and baby seats in the back, but Mio reached for Primo with a practiced air.

The toddler, who'd discovered Evans' iPhone in his pocket, played with it. Evans let him hold onto it. It was turned off. He watched Primo succumb to being put in his seat. Primo reached for the snap securing his mini-seat belts. Mio buckled him in, kissing the little boy's head.

"He's done this before," Evans said with a smile.

Belen busied herself putting Violeta into her carrier.

Mio turned to him. "*Bésame,*" he whispered. "Kiss me."

Their kiss was sweet but brief.

Belen caught them, and Mio grinned. "You mind sitting in the back?" he asked Evans as he slipped on aviator-style shades.

Oh, he was a hot and sexy man. Evans did mind, feeling a bit like Cinderella, but he wanted to make a good impression on Belen and Primo.

"I live for the backseat," he said, throwing himself beside Primo.

"Now we drive home, and you'll see Las Ramblas and the living statues," Mio said.

Beep. Holy heck. Somehow, Primo had unlocked Evans' cell phone and was playing with the telephone keypad. He climbed into the car beside the boy, who resisted giving up the phone. Evans pressed a couple of buttons and produced his new favorite thing. A mini keyboard.

Primo gave him a dazzling smile and busied himself with his new toy. They peeled away from the curb, baby Violetta kicking her feet as a happy samba played.

"Wow, he's good." Evans was impressed.

"He's going to be a DJ," Mio said over the sound.

Belen laughed. "His father wants him to be a matador."

Evans balked at the idea. He loved animals and hated cruelty toward them. He'd already told Mio not to even *think* about taking him to a bullfight.

"Oh-oh," Mio said. "Evans loves bulls. No matadors for him."

"I don't like bullfights either," Belen said.

"You just like to eat meat," her brother joked, and she punched his arm playfully.

Evans suddenly wondered where they were headed. He hadn't really thought beyond arriving here and being with Mio. He hadn't expected a family greeting. He wondered if he and Mio would be saying alone together . . . or did he live with his family?

"Here is Las Ramblas," Mio said over his shoulder as they entered a beautiful, leafy promenade with gigantic plane trees lining the middle of the road.

"Turn that thing off, Primo." Belen reached back, grabbing the cell phone out of her son's hand. The sound muted, Mio no longer had to shout above the music.

Primo's eyes pooled with tears.

"Here," Evans said, scrambling for his earphones. He took the phone back from Belen, plugged the cord into the unit and put the earbuds in Primo's ears.

35

"What an actor," his mother said as tears kept falling down his little face.

Primo smiled again as Evans mopped his tiny face and got the music going again. Evans felt a swell of emotion when he caught Mio's searing gaze in the rearview mirror.

Squawk!

Primo started imitating the sounds from the side of the road. Large cages, feathers falling from some of them onto the ground shook as the car roared past.

"What is in those cages? What kind of birds?" Evans leaned forward, peering at the crazy, colorful sweep of street.

"Exotic birds," Belen said. "Our city has a long way to go with animal rights. You can buy them as pets... hey... look over there at the food stalls. You can even buy insects to eat."

"Are you kidding?"

Mio laughed. "No. But mi madre is cooking. Big lunch. No insects for you today."

Evans stared at the human statues surrounded by tourists. "That's supposed to be the Statue of Liberty?" He pointed toward a man covered in gold foil and caked in what looked like clay.

"Some of these people have been coming here for years. They do this every day. It's how they make their living. Hey, we can stop for a moment." Mio swerved to the side of the road.

"You need to watch for pickpockets," he said. "Don't keep your wallet in your back pocket. Belen, hold your purse close."

"I know, I know, you're such a papa."

Mio snapped his fingers. "Primo."

The toddler scrambled out of his seat, dropping Evans' iPhone beside him as he jumped into Mio's arms. Evans quickly picked it up, wondering if his bags were safe in the trunk.

As the small family wandered through the weird and wonderful assortment of people, Evans felt his ass being fondled.

"Not a pickpocket." Mio grinned. "Only me."

Evans laughed. Primo sat atop Mio's shoulders and held his little hand down to Evans, who was touched that the toddler wanted to hold his hand.

There were flowers everywhere. Mio hadn't been kidding. Roses were in full bloom in buckets and baskets, their heady smell intoxicating.

"Did Mio tell you about La Díada de Sant Jordi?" Belen asked.

"He mentioned it. What is it?"

"It's the Barcelona version of Valentine's Day. It is the most sacred day of lovers." She grinned. "Don't worry. I'll let you know everything in plenty of time, but you will see roses everywhere since it is coming in thirteen days. Primo, don't eat the lady's hat!"

They had approached a couple dressed as bowls of fruit. Primo reached down from Mio's shoulders, tugging at some grapes perched high on what looked like a bowl but was actually a woman's hat. The lady laughed as her head poked over the top of a gaudy, fruit-filled street barrow. Beside her, a man laughed, pulling her out of Primo's determined grip.

"They are I think, very popular," Mio said. "They have been doing this for nine years. Longer than anyone."

Evans was particularly touched by the couple painted in blue, sitting on a park bench kissing. They barely moved a muscle until they had a crowd around them, then the movement was only to tilt their heads closer.

"Oh, that man is dressed like Don Quixote!" Evans felt a delirious sense of joy at recognizing the whimsical suit of armor and the lance of an elderly man posing close by.

"That's right," Mio said. "You being a writer would know that." He reached squeezed Evans' butt again. He was driving Evans crazy.

Primo slipped down from Mio's shoulders and into Evans' arms. Mio looked surprised.

"He likes you." As Primo's attention was taken by a man covered in pigeons, Mio kissed Evans' ear and said, "I think we might fight over you."

Evans laughed again. Out of the corner of his eye, he saw a couple of guys pointing at somebody. He followed their gazes, surprised to find it was Mio. Yes, he was hotter than hell, but the surreptitious way one of them pulled out a camera phone and took a photo of him was an even bigger surprise. The two men quickly moved on. Had he imaged they were taking photos of his lover?

"We should go," Mio suddenly said, checking his watch. "*Mi madre* . . . she will be expecting us."

Evans couldn't help feeling apprehensive about meeting Mio's parents.

"Come," Mio said, and they returned to the car, narrowly missing another parking ticket. They zoomed away from Las Ramblas, toward the hills.

"I warn you, my family's crazy," Mio shouted.

Evans smiled. *Baby, you don't know crazy like I know crazy.* He wondered how Nora was doing and shut her out of his mind.

They took a pretty drive along a winding, coastal road, Evans trying to drink it all in. It was a beautiful city. They passed a sign saying Horta-Guinardo.

"This is where we live," Belen said over her shoulder. As they drove, Evans watched the colorful flow of houses and apartments. Peach and beige seemed to be the predominant choice of paint color, and he loved the bright red roofs. Mio turned on the radio, and happy Flamenco-style music played.

For a moment his gaze held Evans' in the rearview mirror. It was a look that promised so much that Evans felt his cock hardening. They turned up more winding roads, and Evans saw shop owners closing their doors.

"Why are they closing up?" he asked, yelling over the music.

"It's siesta time," Belen shouted back.

"Until four-thirty or five, a lot of people close their shops for lunch and a siesta. It's a tradition that started many years ago. We still do it."

A man paused outside a small shop, and Mio stopped beside him, giving him a finger wave. The man stared at them as Mio powered on.

"I love that tradition," Evans yelled back as they stopped outside a three-story house that he soon discovered belonged to the Cortez family.

"We live on the top two floors," Belen told him. "We rent the bottom floor out to two other families."

The smell of olive oil and garlic carried on the breeze, and he started to salivate. He'd eaten well on the flight, but now he was starving.

Mio took possession of Evans' belongings as they mounted some stairs at the side of the house. Evans held Primo, who put his little head on Evans' shoulder. The child was utterly endearing.

Belen opened the door at the top of the stairs.

A burst of Spanish came from inside. He could pick out *padre* — father — and then an exchange of words between Mio and, Evans assumed, his mother.

"She's mad because Mio didn't stop to pick up our father, but he's supposed to get exercise," Belen said.

"Wait . . . that was your father on the street?"

Belen nodded. "My father and Mio . . . they . . . you know . . ." She moved her hand in a back and forth gesture. This was a surprise. Mio never let on he didn't get along with his father. Now he was even more nervous.

Mio's mother came running from the kitchen. She was a funny, feisty woman who hugged Mio, Belen and the children, and threw herself at Evans, who laughed as she pinched and kissed his cheeks.

"Aren't you going to tell her you can't live without her?" Belen asked, and in spite of his flood of worries, Evans laughed.

"*Estoy encantado de conocerte,*" he said.

"*¡Bueno!¡ Bueno!*" Mio's mother shouted an inch from his face, touching and squeezing his cheeks as if testing a tomato for ripeness.

"Very good. You are learning Spanish," Mio said.

Evans was relieved he'd managed to get *I am pleased to meet you* right.

"Come, I'll show you to your room," Mio said, shooting off to the right.

Belen took Primo out of Evans' arms. "Lunch is ready," she shouted at Mio.

"I know," he shouted back, rushing into a room that overlooked the leafy green neighborhood. Evans took in the double bed, chest of drawers, a small table by the bed, and not much more.

Mio closed the door behind Evans, dropped his bags on the floor. He shoved a chair under the door handle.

"Pants down," he said.

"But—"

Mio made a *tsk* sound and pushed Evans to the bed. There was a grim look on his face as he unfastened the buttons on Evans' jeans, gripped the sides, and yanked them down. He let out a cry when he saw how hard Evans was and his eyes glazed over with pure lust.

Evans lay in a moment of wonderment, unable to move. His hands rested by his sides as he watched his lover's mouth move over his boxer briefs.

I can't believe how he looks . . . at me!

"Mio!" His mother's voice rang out, but Mio was too far gone, liberating Evans' cock from his briefs. He grasped the cockhead with his fingers, a look of delight crossing his face.

"*Mía*," he said. Evans knew this meant *mine* and almost came right there in Mio's hand except that his lover gripped his cock hard. "Turn around. On your knees."

Evans lost no time in turning over and steadied himself on all fours. His jeans pooled at his knees. Mio fumbled with the button and zipper of his own jeans, then stroked his fingers possessively across Evans' ass cheeks. Evans heard the sharp intake of breath as Mio's tongue invaded his ass, licking and sucking at Evans' hole.

Mio's hands held Evans' ass in his hands, separating the cheeks with his thumbs. He spat on Evans' hole, surprising him.

"Fuck me," Evans muttered as little Primo banged on the door.

Mio took his face away, gripping Evans to him. Evans felt the huge, hot cock poking at him. Mio was uncut, and Evans loved to tease the hooded shaft with his lips and tongue. He longed for it, but there was no time now. He felt the glistening, moist head push past the foreskin, jutting at his ass hole.

"I couldn't wait to breed you." Mio rasped.

Please, oh please. He wanted to scream for it, but Mio's right hand shot around to Evans' cock again, squeezing off pre-come and spreading it on Evans's hole. He shoved his cock inside Evans hard and deep, both hands holding Evans exactly where he wanted him. His hips slapped against Evans's ass and thighs.

"Come, guapo," he urged. "Come for me."

Evans came hard, his breath sticking in his throat. He fought for air as Mio's hand moved back to Evans' erupting cock.

He took himself out of Evans, and the battering at the door continued.

"No!" Evans wanted to scream, but his voice came out a low moan. Mio caught Evans's juices in his hand, rubbed it over his cock, the slippery sound exciting Evans even more. He turned and watched his lover enter him again, and his ass muscles clamped down on Mio.

Mio's mouth pursed into a satisfied smirk. Evans reached back for a kiss. Mio's mouth descended on his, his tongue stroking the inside of Evans's mouth as his cock erupted in Evans's ass. Both men sighed. It was over far too soon.

"Welcome to Barcelona, guapo," Mio said against Evans's ear. "Delicious tapas. Now I want lunch."

He lightly slapped Evans's ass as he pulled away from him. They re-dressed quickly.

"I like feeling you all over me," Evans said.

Mio kissed him. "Good."

Out in the hallway, Primo came charging at them, raising his arms to Mio, who hoisted him up.

"The little monkey will open your door early in the morning. So make sure you put the chair against the door when you go to bed tonight, eh?"

"What do you mean?" Evans followed him toward the kitchen, which opened to a huge family dining room. "Aren't you going to be with me tonight?"

Mio either didn't hear him or chose to ignore him.

The lunch table was crowded with people. Mio introduced his father, who nodded a greeting, waving his fork around as if that might lure some food onto his plate. Mio seated Primo in a special child-size seat on top of one of the chairs and kept up a running introduction of various relatives at the table.

"Sit here," he told Evans, who felt their curiosity but soon became aware that Mio's mother had kept lunch waiting for his arrival. He watched plates whiz around the table, and occasionally somebody plopped a spoonful of something on his plate.

Mio's mother nudged him. "*Comer.*" She mimed eating.

He was seated between her and Belen, who whispered, "Lunch is our biggest meal. You should eat now. It's a long wait until dinner."

Evans tucked into tasty portions of aubergine, fresh salmon, and mussels soaked in garlic and white wine. He noticed everybody sopping up the rich juices with dense, fresh bread, and did the same. Mio's mother put some soup in front of him, and he almost swooned over the homemade corn and tomato soup.

"I can taste all the vegetables," he said to Belen. "Even the parsley."

Belen smiled. "She grills each vegetable, even the parsley."

Baked chicken and potatoes came next. Evans scooped up some green beans that arrived on his plate drizzled with olive oil and lemon. He'd never had a better meal in his life.

Even the children ate with gusto. It wasn't anything like the sedate meals he was used to, but it was wonderful. Mio's mother put a platter of fruit and a bowl of ice cream on the table.

Mio lost interest in the meal and sat back, playing with his cell phone. Evans was surprised to see him texting. He never texted Evans and always said he hated text messages. Mio left the table and Evans watched him outside through the huge picture windows, muttering into his phone, one hand gesticulating wildly. Evans had never seen him so angry.

Evans heard him yelling, but didn't understand the words. He picked out *not now*, but that was all. Mio returned to the table, looking furious. He lifted his glass of wine and downed what remained, his angry gaze connecting with Evans. He tilted his head to the right, beckoning Evans to follow him.

"Excuse me," Evans said, hurrying away from the table. "What's going on?" he asked Mio when he caught up with him in the hallway.

Mio barely looked at him as he strode to the front door.

"I have to go to work. Something's come up . . . only *I* can take care of it."

"Okay . . . well, um . . . that's okay, I understand. We can do something later, right?"

Mio gave him an odd look that Evans couldn't decipher.

"No." His tone was terse, and it didn't improve. "I'll be working very late. I have no idea when I will finish. You stay here tonight. I'll see you tomorrow."

"*Tomorrow?* Are you kidding me? It's four o'clock in the afternoon!" Evans couldn't help venting a little frustration. "You're working through the night?"

Mio's eyes narrowed. "Don't question me. This is business."

Funny business. "What is it that you have to do exactly that's going to take all night?"

The chill of communication shutdown shocked him. He'd never experienced Mio shutting him out like this.

"I'm not going to explain myself here. I didn't say I will work all night. I will finish late and stay at my apartment."

"Your apartment? You mean you don't live here?"

"No, I don't live here."

"Why can't I stay at your place while you're working? I want to be with you, Mio. I—"

"I told you *no*. You will be all alone, and there's nothing for you to do there. At least here you have company." His voice dropped. "And I don't want Belen to be alone."

"But Mio—"

"I have to go now."

Mio picked up a jacket from a peg by the door and left, without even turning around to glance at him. Evans leaned against the wall, feeling empty and stupid.

What the hell have I done coming here? I should be home looking for a job . . . instead, I'm here to be with a man who takes off and leaves me with a bunch of people I don't know.

As he heard Mio's car start and the squall of tires, he closed his eyes.

Who the hell is this guy? What could he be doing all night? Why did he ask me to come here?

CHAPTER FOUR

"Well, let's look at this thing logically. The possibilities are endless . . . and fascinating, you gotta admit. My money's on him being a hit man."

"Don't be ridiculous." Evans scoffed at Michael's words, but the truth was, anything was possible. He hoped his lover wasn't a trigger-happy killer, but he really had no idea.

"Mio's always played his cards close to the chest, and I probably should have pressed more but . . . but . . ." The only things Evan knew for sure were that he felt wretched and excluded. He paced Mio's family's backyard, talking to Michael on his cell phone.

"You were in Camp Happy Cock, and it's understandable," Michael said.

Evans was relieved Michael wasn't encouraging him to hop a plane back to L.A. Only a true friend would talk him off the ledge this way.

"Maybe he's an undercover cop," Michael suggested. "He could be a spy or a drug dealer, but dealers make quick drops . . . can't imagine he's involved with some big deal that would take all night. Hey, maybe he's a drug enforcement agent?"

"Well, that narrows things down a little," Evans said.

Michael giggled. "Maybe he's a stripper."

"I don't know why he hasn't told me . . ." *Boy, he must have something big to hide.*

"We should have done a Google search before I let you get on the plane," Michael said. "I was too busy being mad at you."

"I tried doing that and couldn't find anything on him."

"You did? When?"

Evans blew out a sigh. "When I first met him. I couldn't find anything at all, but I figured since the guy lived in Spain, maybe he wasn't into networking sites like we are in the States."

"Honey, I hear you. You know my niece has a Facebook page, and she is only seven months old."

Evans laughed. "I know. And your dog has one, too."

"Everybody has a Facebook page," Michael retorted. "Anybody who is anybody has a Facebook page."

"Not everybody," Evans retorted. We both know plenty of people who don't."

"And they're weirdos. Give me your guy's name again. Hey . . . what about the family address? Give me that, too. You said he has a sister. What's her name?"

"Her name is Belen, and something's going on there. Mio doesn't want her to be alone. I don't have an actual street address. They live in the suburb of Horta. Wait a minute . . . I saw a street name."

"Get it for me," Michael said.

Evans let himself out of the side gate, ran down the stairs and onto the street.

"Carrer de Mercedes," he said, squinting up at the sign. A pale green bird that looked like a mourning dove except for its coloring, perched atop the sign, peering down at him.

"Mercedes, like the car?" Michael asked. He could hear Michael pounding on the computer keyboard. "How . . . elegant. Parents' names?"

"No idea. I don't think Mio said." Evans heard the clatter of little feet. Belen and Primo came out of the house toward him. "Hey, I gotta go. Call me if you get something, yeah?"

"I will. And hang in there. I think this guy's crazy about

47

you."

"Thank you, Michael." Evans was touched. Sometimes Michael could be a total sweetheart.

"Happy trails," his assistant said and ended the call.

"Are you okay?" Belen asked him.

"Yes, thank you."

Primo clung to his leg. He had something sticky in his hand. Pie. When Evans tried to pick him up, the little boy ran from him, darting across the road, hiding behind a tree. Primo peeped around the tree trunk and shrieked with laughter when Evans ran after him. Playing hide and seek with Primo lifted his spirits and as Evans collected the little boy into his arms, Belen watched with a sweet smile.

"Don't worry," she said, putting her hand on his arm. Evans felt his spirits drop again. "Mio . . . he is crazy about you."

"You heard us talking?"

She lifted her shoulders. "Mio is very . . . you know, private. Come on, Primo, we wash your hands and go to the park."

Evans walked back to the house with them. "What does he do for a living?"

She smiled again. "He has a business."

"Yes . . . I know." Damn! Is that all she knows?

"It's nothing . . . bad," she whispered as they walked into the house.

Mio's mother rushed over to him, grabbing his hand and taking him back to the table where coffee and pie awaited him. He wasn't really hungry anymore, but he didn't want to offend her. Surprisingly, the pie was so good it improved his mood.

"Mmmm . . ." he said.

Mio's mother grabbed his face and kissed his cheeks.

"What is it? Um . . . *qué es lo*?"

She clapped her hands and laughed.

"My mother loves when you speak Spanish," Belen said, patting his head.

As Mio's mother burst forth with rapid-fire words, he tried to interpret them.

"I know it's custard," Evans said, "but what is the fruit?"

"Cherries, very sweet cherries. They grow locally," Belen told him. "We're very proud of them."

"I've never tasted anything quite like them." He took another bite and laughed when Mio's mother smothered him with kisses again.

Belen swung Primo toward the kitchen sink. "*Mi madre* likes you," she said over her shoulder.

And he liked Mio's mom. He liked all of them. He found comfort in Belen's words that Mio wasn't involved in something bad, but still hated how their exchange had gone down. He swallowed his coffee as Belen prepared the children for a visit to the park. Remembering that Mio said he didn't want his sister to be alone, he got up to join her.

"Are you sure?" she asked.

He nodded. He caught, he was certain a glimpse of relief in her eyes and wondered what her story was. This family was full of mysteries. He thought about his own and realized he had a few of his own.

Mio's mother said something in rapid-fire Spanish and Belen smiled.

"She says we should leave the children. They're ready for a siesta anyway. My father wants to nap . . . we'll take the car and go to the Barri-Gotic area. It really is very beautiful."

"Sure," Evans said. "I'm all yours."

Belen took her father's stately Citroen out of the garage. "He likes to drive it on Sundays," Belen told him. "He runs the little café and grocery store down the street. He owns it with his brother. They take turns behind the counter, otherwise, they argue."

Evans laughed. "What do they do the days they're not working?"

"Ah, they sit, they drink coffee, and each tells the other one what to do."

He liked Belen. She had a wonderful sense of humor. They headed back toward the city and Belen seemed younger, more carefree as they lowered the windows and cranked up the music.

"Are you married?" he asked her.

"Sí." Her smile dimmed for a moment. "Oooh . . . I love this song."

Evans heard didgeridoo and drums. "I bought this CD on the streets of the Barri-Gotic. These musicians play there all the time. I hope they are there today," she said, bopping along to the music.

They found parking off Las Ramblas and walked along the street. Evans was mesmerized by the tall, gothic buildings and tiny, narrow streets that made up the old gothic quarter.

"Barcelona was built during the height of the Roman era. The ancient forum where they had many trials was up on the hill there." Belen threaded her arm through his and pointed ahead.

"The Barri was a city within walls, with a river used for trade. Most of the original Roman wall is gone, some of it remains. In this neighborhood, Picasso lived here for many years before he died. Some of the buildings go back to Roman times, some from the tenth century. There are buildings from the seventeenth and eighteenth centuries.

"Ah, this street is my favorite, Tapineria. It is named for a type of shoe women wore in the middle ages. They were tall shoes made of cork, and they had cloth coverings. This whole street used to be shoemakers."

They paused to look at the tiny boutiques and stores selling everything from baked goods to clothing.

"Sometimes," she said, "I am certain I can hear little hammers still making those shoes."

He smiled at her. He could almost hear those little hammers himself.

"See this wall? It is the backbone of the Barri-Gotic, part of the Roman wall. It is beautiful, no?"

"Very beautiful." They twisted and turned down tiny alleys alive with voices and music. "It's like a labyrinth."

"Exactly," she said. "That is what we call it."

The entire district was impressive. He loved the cathedral, which was truly a vision of gothic splendor. The movie-maker in him immediately began plotting an intricate murder mystery set inside the antique walls.

"This street here is The Call. It is a sad chapter of our history. It used to be the Jewish neighborhood. In 1391 there was a riot. So many of the Jewish people were killed. They were all driven out of here in the end."

"Wow," he said. "Every country has its shameful histories, I guess."

"This is true." She pointed our architectural detail in the lovingly-preserved buildings that all housed contemporary stores now but had lost none of their originality. He was just pleased to see no big American chain stores among them. It gave the area a very authentic vibe.

He stopped when he saw the sign Angel Square.

"What is this?" he asked her. "It feels . . . familiar."

"There used to be the statue of an angel here. It was moved to the museum here in Barcelona. This is where Saint Eulalia was crucified, and at her death, people said an angel appeared. They said it was Saint Michael."

Evans was overcome with emotion, a sense-memory—a feeling of white doves—and was not surprised when a couple of them appeared in the square.

"Was Saint Eulalia ever associated with doves?" he asked her.

"It's interesting you should ask that. Her death was very gruesome, especially for a young girl. She was thirteen when she became martyred. They cut off her breasts, stuck her in a barrel with knives, crucified her . . . and finally, they decapitated her. Witnesses said a dove flew out of her head when she was decapitated."

He had always loved a painting he'd once seen in a coffee table book of Saint Eulalia, by John William Waterhouse. The painting haunted him. At the time, he'd been visiting friends and studied the pale, delicate picture for hours. He remembered now or thought he remembered white doves in the piece. He remembered other birds . . . pigeons? But he remained haunted by doves, the messengers of peace and love.

"She's the patron saint of Barcelona," Belen said.

"I never knew that. I have seen a painting of her, and it haunts me."

Belen smiled. "You're in for a surprise soon. I won't tell you now, but you'll soon see."

Somehow, the young saint's trials deepened his inexplicable attachment to the Barri-Gotic, and he was thrilled Belen had brought him here. She knew each building and each street very well.

"This street, Traginers, this is where the mule drivers lived."

Evans laughed. "Really?"

She nodded. "Many lived in rooms above the mule stables."

They walked under archways, above which little latticed windows shone in the sun. It filled him with wonder and a sense of peace. He expected to hear horses' hooves not the roar of motor scooters, but somehow it seemed right.

"See this store right here? This was once a stable. They lived and worked here, fighting for crumbs. They used mules for everything back then, and many of them shared their own food with their mules . . . to keep them alive, to keep themselves employed. Oh, look at this. This is where the city was once walled, keeping the river out."

Belen suddenly grimaced. "I must be boring."

"No, not at all. Who is this street, Avinyo named after?"

"A poet knight from the fifteenth century."

"Belen," he said. "Are you a writer?"

She laughed. "Sí. I am a writer."

"What kind of things do you write?"

She flapped her hands. "Nothing you would want to read."

"How do you know? I'd like to see something you've written."

"I write . . . you know . . . romances."

He smiled. "Have you sold any?"

Her eyes widened. "I haven't tried. My husband said I am wasting my time, but Evans, I love to write. I *need* to write."

He hugged her then. "I want to read your stories. Are any of them set in Barcelona?"

When she nodded, he became convinced he could help her. He had a friend who owned a publishing company that specialized in romance novels and always wanted exotic locations. If Belen could even vaguely write, he would steer her in the right direction.

They sat at one of the few empty tables at a pretty, tiny outdoor café on a terrace surrounded by high stone walls. He had a giddy moment when he thought of himself as a centurion ordering a meal, from a servant. Some young Irish musicians played music using empty beer bottles on the stairs below them. They were very talented. He could pick out the tune "Danny Boy," and it made him smile.

"You want to try a *suizo*?" Belen asked.

He nodded, even though he should have been feeling full, plus, he had no idea what it was.

"On the weekends, they have a fruit and vegetable market here," she said. "My children love it."

They listened to the music as accompanied by the drummer from another busker band that strolled by. As the crowd grew around the innovative performers, Evans felt relaxed for the first time since he'd arrived in Barcelona.

The waiter brought them their drinks. *Suizo* turned out to be the richest, most velvety hot chocolate he had ever tasted in his life, topped with thick and delicious fresh cream.

For a moment, neither of them spoke as they spooned the silky cream into their mouths.

Belen's cell phone rang as the musicians took a break. She beamed as she listened to her caller.

"He's right here, Mio." She handed the phone to Evans and winked. "He is upset because you have your cell phone turned off."

"Guapo?" Mio's voice cracked. "Guapo, I am so sorry. I hate that we had a fight. I never want to fight with you. I want only to make love to you."

Evans felt his toes curling in his shoes. "Me, too."

He was certain he heard Mio let out a breath. "I will come by when I have finished my work," he said. "I already miss you."

Evans smiled. "I miss you, too."

Mio seemed reluctant to end the call, but blew kisses in his ear, clearly expecting kisses back. Evans complied, and Mio whispered goodbye.

Belen grinned at him. "I've never seen my brother so . . . so . . ."

He cocked a brow at her.

"*Golpeado*."

"*Golpeado?* What does that mean?"

She slapped her hands together.

"Hit?" he asked her, mortified.

She shook her head. He remembered the small pocket translator dictionary back at the house and pulled out his cell phone. According to babelfish.com it meant *struck*.

"Sí," she said. "*Golpeado violentamente.*"

"Struck violently?"

"Sí. My brother . . ." She mimed someone in a daze, eyes crossed. She pointed at Evans. "He loves you." She reached across the table, and her strong fingers dug into the palm of his hand. "Please . . . please don't break his heart."

Evans opened his mouth and stared at her. He was more afraid of Mio hurting him. He heard a loud clap and turned to see the musicians laughing. He turned back again to find Belen sobbing.

"Belen, what is it?"

She shook her head and swatted at her tears with the tiny paper napkin under her cup. "Nothing . . ."

"I'm here. I have nothing else to do but listen. And I have no judgments."

She shook her head and pressed her lips together as if to stop herself from responding.

"Tell me." Evans rubbed his thumb across the soft skin on the back of her hand.

"I wish my husband would call me. I don't want to be jealous. I wish he misses me."

"Where is he?" He kept his voice soft, stroking her hand. He didn't want to break contact, he didn't want to do anything to break the spell.

"He's here in Barcelona. I left him because he drinks. I wish he loved me more than he loves wine."

Her confession was shattered by the sound of a bottle breaking. Somebody swept up the broken glass at the foot of the stairs. Poor Belen's frayed nerves seemed to get the better of her. She covered her face with her hands. Evans threw some euros on the table and led her away from the noise . . . and the glass.

They left the old quarter, Belen in a subdued state. He knew she regretted telling him the truth.

"My sister takes drugs," he said.

She shifted her gaze from the cobblestones to Evans's face. "Oh, I am sorry."

"Mio never told you?"

She shook her head. A faint smile touched her lips. "Mio . . . he is very private."

"Well, she is in the hospital, and she needs a lot of help. I hate to see her like that."

Belen nodded. "My husband . . . he likes the drugs, too. When he drinks, he takes drugs . . . when he takes drugs, he . . ." Her face crumpled.

"Does he hit you?"

"Not yet." Her voice was a whisper. "He throws things. It is bad. It was hard for me, but I took our babies, and I left him."

They reached the car.

"He hasn't tried to come back . . . to be with you?"

She shook her head. "I think he is busy having parties at our house."

"Oh, Belen, I'm so sorry."

They got into the car, and she fired up the engine. "What drugs does your sister take?"

"Cocaine."

She looked shocked. "Same as Gilberto." She bit her lip. "He gets . . ." She twirled a finger around her ear indicating *crazy*.

"My sister, too."

As they headed back home, he put his hand on the back

of Belen's neck. She dropped her shoulders instantly. It had a calming effect on her it seemed, and he kept it there. She turned off the CD and found a classical flamenco music station.

"I always wanted to be a dancer." She smiled again. "A dancer . . . a writer . . . and a mama. One out of three is good, no?"

"It's very good. I want to talk to you about your writing."

She told him she would let him read some of her stories and seemed lighter and happier as they talked about their favorite writers and favorite movies. Safe topics for troubled souls.

He spent a wonderful evening with the family. Jet lag had hit him around five o'clock, but he powered through it. He knew he had to stay awake and sleep on Barcelona time or else he would struggle for days with it. There was no word from Mio, and Evans found the kids fully occupied his time. He helped Belen bathe them after dinner, and he sat on the back porch with Mio's parents as she tucked them into bed.

They heard Primo crying.

"Oh, he misses his papa," Mio's mother said. Her sad eyes gazed up at the moon.

"Does he come to visit the children?" Evans asked her, using his Spanish-English dictionary. He had no idea if he sounded clumsy, but she seemed to understand him.

She shook her head.

They could hear Belen's lovely voice as she sang, *"Duermete lucerito de la mañana, de la mañana."* Her voice was true and pure.

"I sing this song to my children when they were babies." Mio's mother pointed to the sky. "It is a full moon, a time for dreams. A time for sleep."

Her English was better than he thought it was.

She and her husband went to bed, leaving Evans alone with his thoughts. When Belen came and joined him on the porch, he asked her what the song was.

"*The Little Bird That Sings.*" She smiled. "I am going to sleep now. I had a wonderful day. Thank you." She gripped his hand for a moment.

"I'm going to bed, too," he said.

Belen kept singing softly to herself.

"What does that line mean?"

Her eyes shone in the semi-darkness. "Sleep, my little morning star. Whatever happens, Gilberto gave me two shining stars. I love them very much."

I know you do." They hugged each other and went to their own rooms. He wished he could sleep, but he felt restless. He had passed the sleepy apex of his jetlag and was now wired.

He found the European adaptor for his laptop and was figuring out the buttons and switches to get it working when he heard the soft tap of a car horn honking. He heard it a second time. It couldn't be Mio, could it?

His cell phone rang next.

"Guapo . . . come out now. I have a couple of hours. Let's go."

He abandoned his project and ran outside with his keys and wallet in hand. He almost fell down the stairs in his haste to reach his lover.

"Guapo," Mio said when he saw him. He stood up in the driver's seat and leaned over to kiss him.

"Where are we going?"

"My place," Mio said as their hungry mouths collided.

Evans recoiled, shocked. "Mio . . ."

"Sí?"

Evans stepped back and then forward again.

Mio dropped into his seat, starting the car. "Get in."

"Get in? Are you kidding me?"

Mio looked up at him. "Sí, get in." He must have realized then that something was wrong. His tone sounded fearful. "Please."

"No. First, you are going to explain why your face smells like a woman's pussy."

"Not here," Mio hissed. "Get in."

Evans hesitated for a fraction of a second and Mio pulled him into the convertible, lurching out of the driveway, holding Evans to him in the front seat.

"You want to know why?" he screamed above the roar of the engine.

The two men struggled.

"Yes!" Evans shouted back. They careened around the corner, and he scuttled to safety inside the car, his foot hitting a tree branch as they took the corner sharply.

"I'll tell you why," Mio screamed. "I'm a whore. Okay?"

"A whore?"

Mio became furious. "Yes. A whore. I'm a fucking rent boy. You happy now? Man . . . woman . . . I fuck anybody. Okay?"

They almost hit a street sign, and Mio averted catastrophe outside the car. Inside . . . it was a whole other story.

CHAPTER FIVE

A rent boy. Men. Women . . . oh my God.
"You're . . . bisexual?"

"Some of the men I fuck . . . they're bisexual. They like me to fuck their women."

"And you . . . don't mind?"

Evans wondered how fast he could run to the airport. He remembered his stuff was back at the Cortez household. So were his hopeful dreams.

"I fuck anybody if the money is right."

"And do they fuck you?"

Mio sneered. "For *a lot* of money."

Evans felt as if the man he loved had died. He didn't know this person. In the moonlight and under the lamppost, Mio must have read him well.

"I am still the same person. I am still the man who loves you."

He stared at Mio. *You love me?* "Mio . . . I don't know what to say." He rubbed his head, pulling at his hair. He wanted to be out of his body . . . out of his skin. He didn't want this conversation . . . but fuck . . . as Mio's hand crept along his crotch, he still wanted this man. He brushed Mio's hand away.

"Man or woman, it's all the same to me," Mio said. "But . . . I don't love to fuck women, and now I've met you . . . you are all I think about."

"I had no idea. I never guessed . . ."

"Yes, I know."

The car headed back toward the city. Evans took deep breaths. "Where do you live?"

"L'eixample." Mio smiled at him. The name meant nothing to Evans. "The gay district. Guapo . . . please don't be upset. I love you."

Upset? Upset didn't even begin to cover Guapo's feelings on the subject.

They arrived at an upscale, gated building. Palm trees swayed in the softly lit driveway. It made him think of Beverly Hills . . . minus the movie stars.

Evans felt he was having an out-of-body experience as Mio led him by the hand past a tropical-looking lagoon into the entrance of an apartment. It felt cool inside as Mio turned on the subdued lighting. Evans blinked. It was sleek, ultra-modern. It looked expensive. He saw touches of Mio . . . his jacket, his briefcase. He saw a long table along the left wall. A box of chocolates. He stared at the label. *Al Nassma, Dubai.*

He stared at the words underneath. Camel's milk chocolates.

"When were you in Dubai?" he asked, aware that his voice came out soft and dreamy . . . a little scratchy like a vinyl record that needed cleaning.

Mio watched him, hovering near the front door as if he were afraid Evans would make a run for it.

"Three days ago."

Evans almost laughed. "Three days ago? So when we were talking on the phone, you were fucking some Arab prince in Dubai?"

"An Arab banker, actually."

Evans felt sick. "Do you practice safe sex with these people, and are these chocolates really made of camel's milk?"

"Yes, it is camel milk. The chocolates are very good. Half the fat of cow's milk and they have dates and spices in them."

Evans stood, feeling bewildered. He started to sway.

Mio led him to a plush, long white sofa that seemed to mold to his body as Mio pushed him into it. Mio tried to kiss him, but Evans recoiled.

"God . . . wash your face. Please."

Mio crossed the room and opened the shiny white doors to a well-stocked wet bar. Keeping his gaze on Evans, he poured them both a drink from a cut glass decanter.

He edged back to Evans, holding out a cut glass goblet.

"It's cognac. Take a sip. You'll feel better."

Evans took it. He didn't think anything would make him feel better except learning that this was a hoax. The smell of the cognac hit his brain, and he felt sick before he could take a sip.

Mio left the room. Evans took a deep breath and drank, taking a look around him. He admired the man's taste. He took a bigger swig and almost choked.

"Relax." Mio returned, reaching from the back of the sofa to squeeze Evans' shoulder with one hand. "That cognac is two hundred years old. You'll feel it in a minute." Mio's voice remained low.

"A gift from another grateful client?"

Mio didn't respond. He came around the sofa, put his drink on the coffee table, and sat beside Evans.

"Why couldn't you have been a spy?"

"What do you mean?" Mio asked.

Evans shook his head.

Mio leaned closer. He smelled of soap. Evans felt his lover's fingers on his chin. He closed his eyes when Mio kissed him. Damn. It still felt good. Mio's mouth was gentle at first, then more determined. His insistent tongue slipped between Evans's lips and into his mouth, kissing Evans the way he always did, with his whole face and body.

Evans felt, rather than heard his lover's soft groan and melted. He remembered then that Mio had been with other people that very evening. He would be with yet another man later. He tugged himself away from the sweep of the passionate abyss and brought himself back to earth.

"Aren't you going to be running late?"

Mio sighed and moved away from him, snatching his drink from the coffee table. He paced the room. He was wearing a white suit with a black silk shirt. Not what he'd been wearing when he left Evans earlier. Evans realized he was finally absorbing everything and . . . God, Mio looked good.

His lover took a gulp of his drink. He stood at the window, looking out into the darkness, his back to Evans, who glimpsed treetops and faint lighting outside.

"I practice safe sex with most of my clients. Some demand bareback, but they pay a high price for it."

Mio took another swing but didn't turn around.

"They also have to take blood tests, and I make them do it every month."

"What about you?" Evans was very nervous. "You take blood tests, too? We had unsafe sex today, and I feel really stupid now."

This time Mio turned around. "Yes. We both took those tests, remember? There's something else you should know."

"God . . . no. Now what?" His head went back against the sofa cushion.

"Do you want to know?" Mio's voice rasped.

"Yes."

"I've done some porn. I made eleven movies."

Holy fuck.

"I'm retired. I retired two years ago when I realized I could make more money being an escort."

Evans lifted his head from the cushion. "Gay or straight?"

Mio looked pained. "*Querido*. Gay, of course."

Evans felt a jolt of something between pleasure and pain. Mio had called him darling. God, he was torn. He wanted Mio, and he wanted Mio to want him.

"Tell me what is going on in that beautiful head." Mio returned to him. He put the empty glass down on the table and took Evans' hands in his. He turned Evans' hands palms up and kissed them.

"I love you, Evans. I don't know how it happened. I . . . I took this work when I was a single man, and I had no ties. I was very hurt by love. I never, ever thought I would meet someone. And I—"

"Did you use your own name in the movies?"

"No."

"What name?"

Mio went back to kissing Evans's hands. The look on his face when he raised his face was intense. "Jorge Alejandro."

Evans ran the name around in his brain. He'd seen a ton of gay por, but the name wasn't familiar.

"Guapo . . . I wanted to be with you from the first time I saw you. I want this to work. I tried so hard to tell you what I was doing. Belen said I had to tell you, but I thought I would lose you. Some guys like having a porn star boyfriend . . . but you, I knew you were different. I thought maybe . . . you would never find out."

Evans smiled. "You really thought you could keep up a double life?"

Mio shrugged. "When I first invited you, I thought we could stay with my sister. They have a fantastic house. I thought I could keep the clients you know . . . away . . . tell them I was on vacation . . . then she left her husband—"

"Is he involved in your work, too?"

Mio looked confused. "No. Where did you get that idea?"

The cognac had started working its charm. Evans had

ceased to react emotionally to everything.

"So you like the work, and you want to keep doing it."

"Guapo, I thought . . . I am wondering . . . can you . . . you know . . . I am not ready to quit. One day . . . but the money is too good. I control everything I do. I have good clients. Good, clean guys. I love the variety . . . the travel . . . the beautiful places . . . a few of the guys have quirks, but I love it. I love you, too. So I am thinking . . . you should come with me."

"Come with you? Are you crazy?"

"You've been on two trips with me, and we had a great time, didn't we?"

Evans came out of the cognac-induced haze. "You were working when I met you in London . . . and then in Florida?"

"Sí, señor."

Evans thought back to the men at the hotel pool in Miami.

"Those men who came over and spoke to you . . . did they recognize you from your movies?"

Mio nodded. "Guapo . . . I don't want anyone the way I want you. My work does not have to interfere with our lives together."

"It did tonight," Evans pointed out.

Mio nodded. "It did, yes. I had booked a friend of mine for this couple, and he canceled. They pay in advance . . . . .a lot of money. I had no choice."

"Are you seeing anyone else while I'm here?"

"Two people, but I figured you and my sister could spend time together when I have to work."

"Geez, this is . . . sick. But it's . . ."

"What?" Mio's hand moved to Evans's forehead, stroking it in a soothing way.

Evans glanced at him, trying to sort through his thoughts. "You have sex for a living . . . I mean . . . we have such incredible, connected sex. How do you have the energy for me when you fuck for a living?"

"You just said it. We are connected. I never trusted love, and then I met you. I am certain we can do this. I'm so glad it's out in the open. I—"

"Do any of them hurt you?" Evans wanted to know. "Do they do kinky things to you?"

"Nothing I won't let them do. Some of them like me to piss on them. I used to have this one guy who wanted to pee on me, it's not my thing. I like to fuck. My favorite thing is fucking straight guys who think they might be gay."

Christ . . .

Mio looked smug for a moment but must have remembered who he was talking to. He sighed again. "I started the movies because I have a high sex drive, but the sex was . . . you know, bad. Some of the guys in these movies are used up . . . sometimes they are very high. They do it for the money. They're no better than street trade. I liked a couple of the guys though and liked the lifestyle they had. One of them taught me the ropes of being a high-paid whore. He has a drug problem though, so his lifestyle is not as good as mine. I pick the clients I want to fuck . . . they take me to such beautiful places. The best hotels and restaurants. Guapo, I am serious about you being with me. Come with me. Wherever I go, come with me."

"That's absurd. I can't do that."

"Why not?" Mio shot back. "You have problems getting work now, don't you?"

"I—" Evans gaped. "How do you know that? I've never talked about this with you."

Mio paced the room. "I read, and I learn, Evans. I'm serious about you. There isn't a single other man I've met that I have brought into my home . . . my *life*. I know you are a good man and bad things are happening to you. I feel—" He stared at a tiny painting on the wall and turned back to him.

"I think it's no accident, this timing. I don't believe in accidents. This is fate. Don't struggle there. Think . . . .just *think* about maybe having a life here. I don't understand how you can have the number one show one week, and you have every door closed the next, but I know you didn't deserve this."

"No," Evans said, "I didn't. What you say is true, and it's been horrible."

Mio came to him and took his hands again.

"On the one hand, I got more power by producing my own show. They don't tell you though that when something goes wrong, the producer is blamed and the writer, who is also the producer . . . well, the writer suffers for the sins of the producer."

"And his crazy sister." Mio's voice was soft. "You would be so successful here. Such an asset."

"Thank you."

"I mean it. Take the next two weeks . . . longer if you can. I want to see if we can do this. I really do."

Evans got up and walked around the room, yet even as Evans moved away from Mio, the idea appealed to him. He felt Mio moving close to him, taking his hand, sliding the other one around his body, holding his belly, pushing Evans into his body. He could feel Mio's cock hardening at his tailbone.

"God, Mio," he ground out.

"You see what you do to me?" Mio said in his ear. "You see how much I want you, always? When I fuck people, I have to fuck . . . .what I want more than anything is to fuck the one man I need to fuck."

Evans leaned his head back against Mio's shoulder.

"Look at me," Mio said, but Evans felt utter devastation. As much as he wanted Mio and, yes, as much as he realized now he'd fallen in love with the man, his heart ached.

Mio was talking as he turned Evans around to face him,

but Evans felt his world crashing . . . crumbling. His birth parents hadn't wanted him, and now his lover, the one he thought could possibly be it, wanted . . . the whole world, apparently.

"You look so sad, and that makes me unhappy. Please, Evans, please don't be so sad."

"I don't know what to think," Evans said finally as Mio kissed his eyes, his nose and mouth, kept whispering words of love in Spanish. Evans couldn't breathe, couldn't understand a quarter of what Mio said. He fought his own insecurities, squashing the waves of desire. And yet, when Evans looked down, his fingers entwined with Mio's as if they belonged there. Mio kissed him as if they had always been together. Nobody had ever affected him this way, and he wanted it so much he suddenly felt he would die without this man.

"Please, please give me a chance," Mio said. "Let me show you how fun this can be. Let me love you."

"I don't know," Evans said again, but his body betrayed him. Obviously schooled in the language of physical love, Mio lost no time in stripping Evans's clothing and throwing off his elegant suit and shirt. He wore tight boxer briefs under his white suit. Evans once again marveled at his lover's amazing body. He hadn't seen him naked since they'd been in Miami. He dreamed of this man's hard cock, his ripe, juicy balls. His hand cuffed Mio's coc, and it responded.

"You know how to touch me," Mio said and surprised Evans by picking him up and carrying him to his bedroom. His mouth clamped down on Evans's as if to silence any chance of protest. The room lay in darkness as Mio put him across the bed.

"Who did you fuck tonight?" he asked as Mio moved away from him. Evans felt he was close. *Wow, he weaves such a spell on me.* He couldn't have got up and walked out if he wanted.

Mio struck a match and lit candles by the bed. Evans's eyes adjusted to the light. He heard the crackle of wood wick and could smell tuberose. Mio leaned across the bed to light more candles on the other side.

Evans knew from the glass holders, the scent and the crackling that these were DayNa Decker candles. Each one retailed for around seventy dollars back home. Evans counted at least a dozen. The bedroom was a visual feast of silk, wall tapestries, large paintings, and the gorgeous man on the bed crawling across the cream silk duvet toward him. Mio's hands came to Evans's face, and he resumed the potent kiss he'd started in the living room. He seemed to need Evans the way Evans needed him.

They began a long exploration of one another with their tongues. Evans could still feel Mio's seed left in him from their torrid romp earlier in the day. He reached up his hands, no longer caring where Mio had been or who he had been with. He slid down Mio's underpants and felt joy, swift, sorrowful, and consuming desire as Mio lowered his body to his.

"I missed you," Mio said. His eyes seemed to burn as his knees parted Evans's thighs. His cock sought for instant immersion, and he powered into Evans with a cry. He fucked Evans the way he'd fucked him in Miami. It was more than lovemaking. It was supersonic. As he and Mio came together, he felt the way his lover gathered him in his arms and held him in his moment of release. Evans also felt a glimpse of something else.

He couldn't shake the feeling that he was somehow Mio's salvation.

"I have a question for you now," Mio said.

"What's that?"

"How do you know what a woman's pussy smells like?"

The question struck Evans as so funny he laughed. "I fucked a couple of them . . . until I realized I was gay."

"You're not fucking other men?"

"No. Would you be jealous?"

"Of course I would." Mio put another sensual kiss on his mouth. "I want you to think about making a couple of trips with me, as my companion. A couple of the guys like three-somes. We could fuck them together. They could not know we are lovers in real life . . . we would be there for *them*. They pay for everything."

Evans couldn't even respond. The idea of being a high-price call boy with his own private call boy was crazy. Just crazy.

For a long time, Mio lay on top of him kissing him, his cock hardening as their passion deepened again. Mio's cell phone rang in the other room; Mio clearly tuned into it.

"I have to take this."

He left the bed, his big, meaty cock jutting out. Evans sat up on the bed and looked around the room. It looked nice. Very nice. Mio had expensive taste and a lot of style. He noticed a tin of Clement Faugier's *marron glaces*. The candied chestnuts came from Paris. When had Mio visited the city of light?

Evans opened the black tin and smelled the rich vanilla coming from the chestnuts. He picked out one and unwrapped it, savoring the swirl of flavor in his mouth.

"You have a sweet tooth," Mio said, coming back to the room.

"Yeah."

"Good. I do, too. *Querido*, I must go, but I will be back. You want to shower with me?"

Evans hesitated but followed Mio into the bathroom.

The shower was so luxurious with its marbled interior, big sunken tub, and multiple showerheads. Mio soaped Evans under the hot spray with Tom Ford shower gel, which smelled clean and spicy at the same time. Evans realized this was the aroma which he most identified with Mio. They groped each other's cocks, balls, and asses.

"You fucked a woman tonight?" Evans asked.

Mio let go of Evans and turned off the taps.

"I ate her pussy, then I fucked her husband while he fucked her."

Evans was so stunned he couldn't respond.

"Did you need to know this?" Mio's tone turned icy. "Do you feel better knowing this?" He grabbed a towel and rubbed his wet head.

Evans nodded. "Yes. I have a question. How come you're not with them now?"

Mio laughed. "They are a French couple, visiting from Paris and—"

"Is that where you got the *marron glaces*?"

Mio nodded. "My clients love to bring me gifts. They arrived this evening. I was their . . . *aperitif*. They went to a very important business dinner. Now they want their dessert."

"What will you do with them this time?"

Mio swept the towel across his body, pulled on fresh underpants from a drawer in his walk-in closet and put his black silk shirt and white suit back on. He combed back his hair, dabbed on hair gel and looked sexier than hell.

"I will do whatever they want."

"How long have you been . . . how long have they booked you for?"

Mio hesitated. "Three hours. I never spend the night with a happy couple. I leave them . . . satisfied and with happy memories. Will you wait here for me?"

Evans looked down at the floor. "How many times have you seen them?"

Mio shook his head. "You can't be jealous of . . . *them*." He stepped toward Evans. "It will make me feel good knowing you are in our bed waiting for me."

"Am I the only man you are seeing outside of work?"

Mio laughed. "Of course you are. Why do you think I brought you to Barcelona? You think I have a hotel for hot guys here? Guapo, get some rest. I will wake you with kisses."

He squeezed Evans's cheeks the way his mother had. Evans melted all over again. "I feel like I'm being played."

Mio looked at him. "Love should be fun. I play it like music . . . , not a chess game. I know what you need, and I can give that to you, but right now, it's your move. I have to go. You can stay and let me know you want this, too. Or you can leave and always wonder . . ." He shrugged. "I can play chess, but I prefer the cello. I prefer love over mind games."

He already seemed to detach as he said goodbye, checking his watch as he left the apartment.

Evans blinked a couple of times and pondered his next move. He needed to talk. He needed a friend. He ran to the phone.

"Straight for pay? Darling, that is so the new thing for this decade!" Michael shouted over the cell phone. "I knew it, I knew it! I thought he was involved with either sex or drugs. He's got a cool pad, huh?"

"Very cool."

Evans felt stuck not having a car, but then it was almost midnight. He could hear the sounds of people in the building partying. It wasn't unpleasant. It was a reminder that Barcelona was a different animal to Los Angeles. This city was just coming to life. He paced the living room, noticing new and enticing details. A real fireplace with fresh logs in the grate. Mio collected art. And not just any art. He had some interesting pieces, but Evans was stunned to find the Waterhouse painting of Saint Eulalia that he had coveted. It looked to be original.

How could he and Mio have a passion for the same saint? He smiled thinking back to his conversation with Belen. She knew Mio had this painting and knew that Evans would be ecstatic to see it here.

The painting, which he had only seen in art picture books, was stunning. In it, she lay sprawled on the ground at her death . . . and yes, there were doves in the painting. It stood on the wall opposite the fireplace. Above the fireplace itself was a Pedro Alvarez painting he'd seen in an exhibit in Los Angeles. He was familiar with the tragic Cuban artist's work thanks to Michael dragging him to the exhibit.

Alvarez had moved to Spain and wanted to live there permanently but jumped out of a window of his hotel room in Arizona, killing himself just as his first solo show was underway. The painting, *Welcoming the Backward Swimmer,* was one of Evans's favorites. It had been at there . . . and now it was here. It raised a lot more questions for Evans. He now had a fresh list for discussion with Mio.

"I'm relieved he's not a drug smuggler," Michael said. "And I'm glad he's not a street hustler. I do wonder though . . . who helps him with his scheduling? I mean he must keep info on all his clients, their health records, their quirks . . . he can't remember everything about each one."

"You sound like you've put some thought into this," Evans said.

"I have a friend who's a call girl. Remember Katarina?"

Evans thought back to the pretty, slim blonde. "Sure, I remember her."

"I used to run her office. She had five cell phones and four landlines. She lost the plot when she started sniffing coke . . . she did a Nora North. Ooops. Sorry."

"Don't be," Evans said. He was curious what the small picture was Mio had been staring at. It was of two birds flying to freedom from a small cage. It did something to him. Was Mio offering him freedom? His whole adult life had been spent chasing the Hollywood dream. He moved away from the piece, his thoughts racing.

He switched on a light to a room that looked like an office. It was clean and tidy. On one wall a fax machine stood ready. This must be the famous fax machine from which Mio sent him his scorching love notes. Beside it stood a series of credit card machines and a phone in its charger. One drawer at the desk was not quite closed, in spite of a lock being on it.

He moved to the desk, sat in the big swivel chair and opened the drawer.

"Shit," he said.

"What?" Michael asked. "What did you find?"

"Files. Oh, my God. He has all his clients listed in here."

"Told you. But why does he have it on paper? He should have these things in hidden files on his computer."

"I don't know." Evans lifted out the first file. Carlo Bercovici. "Hey, check this out. He's got forms for each of them."

"Do you see a computer there?"

"No. Oh, wait. There's a laptop in a box in the corner. I've seen him with his laptop when he travels, but I don't see it right now. Listen to this. Bercovici is forty, lives in Rome. He likes threesomes. He likes being spanked. He loves being aggressively fucked, and he loves gardenia-scented shower gel. He's married with three kids but takes business trips. He loves white underwear. He doesn't like being kissed, but loves having his cock sucked as he's watching bullfights on TV."

Michael roared with laughter. "Sounds like my kinda guy."

Evans shook his head. "Doesn't like his nipples being

played with."

"No. He just likes a hard dick up his ass. When are they supposed to meet again?"

Evans held his cell phone to his ear with his shoulder as he kept reading.

"Is all of this in English?"

"Yes," Evans turned the page. "God. He's waiting for Bercovici's latest blood test results. Bercovici spoke to him yesterday. He wants to meet Mio in Portofino."

Michael whistled right in Evans's ear. "That's only the most romantic place in Italy."

"Yeah." Evans tried not to feel jealous that Mio would in all likelihood go meet the mysterious and suave Italian in the idyllic town carved into the Lattari Mountains and overlooking Portofino Bay.

"Sorry," Michael said. "Don't mean to trample your already wounded pride, but you gotta admit it's a helluva lot classier than meeting in some chop shop motel on Santa Monica Boulevard. Ooh . . . What did you say his porn name was?"

"Jorge Alejandro."

"I'll look him up. Are you okay, Evans? I know how sensitive you are."

"Yeah, I'm okay."

"It could be worse."

"Yeah."

"Wow. I just Googled his porn name. Honey, he is fine. Does he still look this good?"

Intrigued, Evans looked at the photo Michael sent to his iPhone. "He's even better."

"Then, honey, if I were you, I'd hang onto him with both balls. Buy some handcuffs. Manacles. Whatever it takes. Hey, he wasn't lying about quitting the biz. And I see eleven movies to his credit."

Evans thought about this. "He could be filming under another name. All the gay porn stars do."

"No . . . I see several fan sites dedicated to him. How did we miss this hunk? He's got some impressive hardware there, Evans."

Yeah, Mio did. Evans took a deep breath.

"A lot of his fans are missing him. He's doing some big live show in a couple of weeks."

"He is? Where?"

"Madrid," Michael said. "Hey, you can always run off and get married there. It's the gay Las Vegas, you know. This says it's sold out and it's one night only. Twelve gay porn stars under one roof. Talk about a dog and pony show."

Evans grew quiet. He was reading some handwritten notes he realized were in Mio's hand. Bercovici liked to have Mio bottom for him, bareback. Hence, the blood test requirement. *God, what the hell am I doing dating a whore?*

"What are you reading? Tell me?" Michael asked.

Evans felt dispirited as he repeated what he'd just read.

"Well, he's a hooker, darling. Guys who pay for a retired porn star expect to get their corks off in his butt." A pause. "Don't take this personally, like you're not enough for this guy. I want you to remember you just met him. You could be his Richard Gere, and he's your Pretty . . . er . . . Man."

"Yeah."

"Geez, you know what? I'm not sure if you can handle this, babe. Maybe you should cut bait now."

"I don't want to."

"Then you'd better figure out a way to make it okay for yourself."

"You're right." Evans rifled through other files in the drawer. "You know, he's got them alphabetized. He's got politicians, a couple of major movie stars—"

"Yeah, like who?"

"Jesse Ford."

"Another married guy with kids. All cock lovin' closeteers."

"But they're mostly businessmen. Some of them have these typed up forms with handwritten notes. In English. Some are written in Spanish by hand."

"Hmmm . . ." Michael pondered this. "You told me he learned the ropes from another guy. Maybe he inherited some of his clients."

Evans made notes. This was another question for Mio.

"I'll call you back," he said when he found a file labeled simply, *Guapo.*

Holy shit.

"What did you find?" Michael asked.

"I'll call you back," Evans said again and ended the call. He took a deep breath. Was he the Guapo? Were there others, in spite of Mio's words?

He opened the file. He was the Guapo, thank God. The file contained his travel itineraries to Miami and Barcelona, the original faxes Mio had sent him. Evans's business card had been photocopied to it. He was stunned to see his production record from the International Movie Data Base was in there. According to the date stamp on the top of the page, Mio had printed it off before they met again in Miami. He also found two articles on Nora North, the worst that had been published. Evans also found an interview he had done with *Screenwriter* magazine.

He smiled when he realized Mio had yellow-highlighted words he must have looked up. Verisimilitude. *How apt.* The truth had now come out.

A separate page fell out, and he caught it. It was a color print of a Pedro Alvarez painting, one he'd found hard to examine at the exhibit because it depicted a slaughtered bull, among other images associated with Spanish life. Mio had scribbled something in Spanish along the margin. No, it was English. *Check with Guapo if this is okay.*

It tickled him to think Mio wanted his approval before buying the painting. He was surprised to see a purchase order putting a temporary hold on the piece now at a gallery in Barcelona. Its price tag was hefty.

His cell phone rang and, thinking it was Mio, he answered. It was Michael.

"I've been thinking," Michael said without any preamble. "It's really a bad idea for Mio to have all that stuff in files just sitting in his desk. He really should keep all this stuff in decoded, scanned computer files."

Evans heard a noise at the door. "He's here," he whispered.

"Good luck," Michael said.

Evans felt a moment of panic as he tried to shove everything back in the drawer. Too late. Mio was already there, staring at him as Evans looked up, guilt and shame flushing his cheeks.

"What are you doing?" Mio asked. "What the *hell* are you doing?"

CHAPTER SIX

"I'm sorry. I got curious."

Mio didn't move. His expression remained incredulous. "You broke into my desk?"

"Of course not. The drawer was open. Mio . . . I'm really your guapo?"

"*Tsk.*" Mio shrugged. "I always forget to lock it. And yes, I told you before. It's three o'clock in the morning. Why aren't you in bed?"

"Too busy snooping."

Mio's eyes glinted, their expression hovering on danger. "Yeah, I noticed."

"How was it?"

Mio bristled. "Not bad."

"Did you have to fuck her?"

"Yes. I fucked her safely, in case you want to know."

"How do you really feel about fucking women?"

"I only fuck two, and they are beautiful women. I like to fuck the men better. The men are handsome . . . a body is a body. I'm going to take a shower. Wait for me in bed?"

"Mio, I've been thinking. You should let me put all these files on computer for you. You shouldn't have any of this on paper lying around."

"I'll think about it. I want you to write . . . not be my secretary. Here are the keys. Can you lock up and go wait for me? Please?"

Evans realized Mio was in a strange mood. It wasn't just the surprise of finding Evans at his desk. It was the result of being with the French couple. Had it been a bad experience? He wished Mio would open up more.

He heard the shower running, locked the drawer, and drifted back to the bedroom. Maybe Mio wasn't used to having someone at home waiting for him. Maybe reality wasn't as much fun as the fantasy.

Mio came into the bedroom, his huge cock swinging between his thighs as he toweled off. Evans sat up in bed, drinking in his lover's beauty.

"I love you, Mio."

Mio's gaze was forceful. "I know you do." He tossed the towel onto a chair. "I have been thinking. If you want to organize my files, you can. I don't want anything shredded though. I want proof."

"We can scan everything into encrypted PDF files and hide them in cloud storage. I can even store them on a flash drive . . . maybe even a special chip you can carry on your key ring."

He looked delighted. "You can do that?"

Evans nodded. "Yes." He had a million questions, but he could tell Mio was exhausted. As much as he swaggered, the day must have been long and tiring for him, too.

Mio slipped into bed with him and their kissing was instantly in the inferno range.

"I have a client who hates to kiss," Mio said.

"Yes, Carlo Bercovici."

Mio dropped a trail of lingering licks across Evans's chin. "See, you are learning my business already. Come with me, guapo, please. I am meeting him in Portofino in a couple of days. You come as my partner. He wants a threesome. He wants a man in his ass and one sucking his cock."

"Will it make you jealous to see me with someone else?"

"No. It will be a big turn on."

Mio pulled Evans to him. His cock was hard, the head

peeking out seductively from its hood made Evans drool, but Evans just knew his man needed rest. Mio's arms went around him. Evans put his head on Mio's shoulder, and before he could ask another question, he heard his lover's steady, dreaming breaths.

Evans awoke to the sound of screaming. It took him a moment. Not screaming. Children. He was aware of little feet. Primo! He struggled awake, realizing he was in the bed alone, and threw his clothes on from the night before.

He stepped into the hallway and found Primo driving a red sports car. It was a toy, but not by much. He steered it around Mio's pristine hardwood floors, one arm dangling to the side, just like Mio drove his car. Primo honked him, and Evans laughed, stepping around the tiny speedster. Mio laughed from his vantage point in the open-plan kitchen off the living room.

"Sorry we woke you."

Little Violeta rocked in a swing. She was awake, pumping her fists to music from the sound system on the black and silver wall unit. Evans stroked her foot, and she giggled.

"Did you sleep okay?" Mio asked, handing him coffee.

"Yes, thank you. What time is it?"

"Nine o'clock. My sister went to the gym for a workout. Then it's our turn. If you want to come with me."

"I need to change."

Mio nodded.

"All my things are at your parents' house."

"We'll get everything from there today."

"This is nice that you watch the babies for her."

Mio smiled. "I am a nice guy, didn't you know? Sorry I fell asleep last night."

"That's okay."

Mio reached out and brushed Evans' cheek then returned

to the kitchen. "Who wants breakfast?"

Primo honked Evans and flipped him the bird.

Mio laughed. "He's a typical Spanish driver."

Evans sipped his coffee. "You made me a cappuccino?"

"Of course, guapo. I have to keep you happy."

Evans walked into the kitchen. The second Primo's back was turned, Mio kissed Evans, slipping him some tongue.

"Man, I could get used to this." Evans reached for a small sweet roll on a plate.

"My father baked these this morning."

Primo blasted his car horn.

Mio didn't skip a beat. "Primo, don't honk your sister."

Primo circled his sister, whose gummy joy soon turned into tears.

Mio rushed around to pluck the toddler out of the car and held him over his head. Primo screamed his joy as Mio tossed him in the air over and over again.

Violeta's sobs tore at Evans. He put his coffee down and ran to her side, unbuckling her from her swing seat. Holding her gently in his arms, he smiled down at her, and her pitiful tears turned into a full-scale scream.

"Oh, my God."

"Jiggle her!" Mio called out as he played with Primo, now running around the room.

Evans jiggled the baby, who balled her fist in her mouth. Primo gave her the finger and Mio grabbed him, tossing him in the air again.

Violeta's ear-piercing shrieks subsided as Evans rocked her in his arms. She stared up at him, hiccupping, her little feet dangling over his arms. He held her closer, against his chest. She nestled into him, and from some distant memory, instinct led him to stroking and patting the baby's chest.

"She's hungry," Mio said. Primo was back in his car now, zooming around the room.

Mio took a warmed bottle out of the microwave and held his arms out for the little girl.

"Evans," Primo sang out. As Mio dealt with bottle-feeding, Evans returned to the living room. Primo wasn't in the car. He sensed movement behind the sofa. A little face peeped out.

"Primo, where are you?" he sang out.

Soft giggles gave the child away, but Evans pretended to look in the armoire, under a chair, even in a drawer.

The little boy's giggles grew louder.

"Primo, are you in here?" Evans jiggled the drawer.

Mio laughed as Primo moved from behind the sofa, making his whereabouts obvious.

"Wait . . . maybe he's behind the sofa," Evans said. Primo squealed as Evans neared him, the little boy laughing as he grabbed his shirt.

The two men played with the babies until Belen returned fifteen minutes later.

She rushed to Evans, hugging and kissing him, and took Violeta out of her brother's arms.

"Thank you both," she said. "Are you coming over for lunch?"

"Of course," Mio said.

Evans went outside and helped Belen buckle the kids into the family car.

"Thank you, Evans." Her hug was fierce. "Thank you for giving my brother a chance." She kissed both his cheeks. "Get him out of this life, and you will make my father a happy man."

"He knows about Mio's work?"

"No. He only knows Mio makes a lot of money and he worries he is in danger. Mio is so mysterious, you know. See you later."

He watched her drive away. Back in the apartment, Mio

was in his office.

"Evans, Carlo has his blood work. He is in good health." He paused, unlocked his desk drawer, and withdrew the Italian client's file. "He wants me to go to Portofino tomorrow. I'd like to tell him I have found a hot man for a threesome. We would travel together. We would be there one night and be back the following day."

"Isn't it a long way to go for one day?"

"No. The flight from here to Rome, where he lives, takes about an hour and a half. He has a private boat that takes us to Portofino, another half hour at the most."

Evans nodded. He forgot they were in Europe and how close so many wonderful cities were.

"He is already there with his wife. We will have our own room on the other side of the hotel. It is a beautiful hotel, one of my favorites. The Il San Pietro di Positano."

Evans stood there listening.

"What do you say?"

"What does it involve exactly?"

"We arrive, he is . . . made aware of this. We have a very nice room. He comes to us, we drink a little champagne. He likes to have sex right away. The first time, I will handle him. Then, after that, we all play. If you don't think you can do it, you can always tell me when the time comes."

Evans blew out a breath. "I've never fucked you. I'm jealous that he has."

"It's not my favorite thing, but you can. Any time you want."

Evans sorted through his emotions once again. "I'd rather be with you than be sitting here wondering what you are doing with him."

"Excellent." Mio was all-business as he handled the flight details. Evans sat opposite him as Mio unlocked a second drawer and withdrew his laptop. He turned it on. Evans was surprised to hear Mio speak fluent Italian on his cell phone. He worked on the computer at a feverish pace.

"The booking confirmation should be coming through." Mio glanced up as the fax machine whisked into action. He leaned over and pulled the incoming sheets out of the tray. Seats 1-A and 1-B on Alitalia Flight seventy-five at seven twenty-five the next morning.

It was heart-wrenching to listen to Mio cooing sweet nothings into the phone. Evans' stomach muscles clenched. He couldn't handle that. How the hell was he going to handle Mio *fucking* another man?

"What would you have told me about your absence tomorrow if you hadn't told me about your secret life?" Evans asked when Mio ended his call.

Mio glanced from the laptop to Evans. "I would have said it's work, which it is, but I ah . . . would have made sure you were okay about it. I always call you from wherever I go." A wounded expression crossed his face. "Never believe the things you hear me say to clients. It's become second nature to me, but seeing how much it hurts you . . ." He lowered his gaze. "I just never thought we'd be having this conversation and I am sorry that my earlier choices have an impact on you now."

"You lied to me," Evans said.

"No, I didn't."

"Yes. You made me believe you're a furniture importer and exporter."

Mio grinned. "But I am, my love. I own a company, and it's my passion, but it doesn't pay the bills. I have a lot of people I have to take care of, and I do it willingly, but selling chairs and coffee tables doesn't do much to establish trust funds for Primo and Violeta. It doesn't put a new roof on my father's house." His gaze rested on Evans' face. "And it doesn't help me spoil you rotten."

Evans opened his mouth and closed it again.

"You feel like a workout?" Mio wiggled his eyebrows at him.

"Sure." Evans wanted to watch his lover in the gym. Maybe they could even sneak in some shower sex.

Mio was in good spirits for their morning workout at Seven, his luxury sports club on Passatge Domingo, in the heart of the gay neighborhood. Guys openly ogled Mio, who smiled at everyone as they took a yoga class. Evans felt critical eyes on him and regretted quaffing half a dozen sweet rolls for breakfast. He felt weird in Mio's borrowed shorts and tank top, but Mio had insisted he had to dress half-naked like the other locals. Mio was in a world of his own as he glided off to work on his upper body in the gleaming weight room.

He might have been aware of the lust-filled gazes and constant whispers, but he didn't make eye contact with anyone, except Evans. He winked at him a couple of times, but it wasn't romantic, merely playful.

They showered separately, and as they dressed again in the locker room, a couple of guys studiously tried making eye contact with Mio, who ignored them. Evans liked the way Mio put a gentle hand on his lower back as they walked out of the gym. He loved everything Mio did.

"I love you, guapo," he said as they got into the elevator.

They were about to exchange a brief kiss, but a couple of guys got into the elevator, too. Mio backed away from Evans, who was glad the elevator ride was only a couple of floors. Out in the car, he asked Mio point-blank why he had avoided contact with him in the gym and elevator.

"I keep my life very private. I like it that way."

"People recognize you, don't they? I noticed that at Las Ramblas . . . as well as in Miami."

"I am nice when people approach me, but I pretend I don't see them. I try not to draw attention to myself, and in Europe, people respect your privacy,"

He turned and looked at Evans as he slipped on his sunglasses. "I feel protective of you, Evans. You have a career back in Hollywood. You have a name. You may not want to be associated with a retired porn star."

"Yes, I do."

Mio's head went back, and he laughed. He reached over and kissed him. "You are so lovely, guapo. I'm so glad I hit on you that day in London."

"Me, too. Hey, what made you do it?"

Mio fiddled with the rearview mirror. "There was something about you. I just . . . I needed to know you."

They headed back to Mio's family house. Evans felt apprehensive about the pending trip, but Mio's good mood continued.

"If you're so worried about my name and reputation, why am I traveling as your companion tomorrow?" Evans asked.

Mio grinned as the wind whipped his hair.

"They don't know that. I book everything myself. My clients don't know my real name. They pay me through a private account, and I handle everything myself. There is no paper trail for their wives to find or their governments . . . you know. They think they're fucking Jorge Alejandro, except I only go by only Alejandro now. I picked the name Everest for you. You like it?"

Evans found himself tickled at the name. "Everest?"

"You are the mountain to me. Nobody comes close. And it is close enough to your name that you will feel comfortable. The boys, they will love you."

"Don't you ever travel by private jet?"

"All the time."

"Then those clients must know your real name."

Mio's smile was disarming. "They do, but they have more to fear from me revealing their secrets than I do."

As they neared the road turning off to his house, they saw Mio's dad standing outside his store, leaning on a broom. He looked right at Mio and Evans and turned away from them, a surly look on his face. Mio took his only hand on the wheel off it to flip off his father's back. Evans bit his lip. Now he knew where Primo had picked up the habit.

At the family house, Mio parked halfway up the sidewalk. "We have lunch and go home and fuck," he said. "We have one nice long siesta."

Evans had no problem with that.

Mio's mother greeted them like returning war veterans, and out of the corner of his eye, Evans spotted Mio giving his mom a wad of cash. She protested in a flurry of Spanish, but Evans sensed it was a show of protest, not a real complaint.

They wolfed down an insane amount of food. Belen and the children arrived late from an outing to the aquarium. Primo held up a stuffed toy, a tiny dolphin, and gripped it through his soup course and as he picked up green beans with his child-size fork.

"Bravo, Primo," his grandmother crooned.

After fruit and creamy, fragrant cheesecake made with nutmeg and honey, Mio caught Evans' gaze. He tilted his head toward the front door. Evans scrambled to his room to pack his things, Belen hard on his heels.

"Why are you leaving?"

"I'm going to stay with Mio."

"When will we see you again?"

"The day after tomorrow, right?" Evans asked Mio as he hunted around for his laptop converter plug. He found it on the floor.

"Yes," Mio said. He continued a conversation with his sister in Spanish.

She took a breath at last. "You promise?"

"Yes, I promise."

"I want to spend time with you," she said to Evans. "I have a couple of stories for you to read."

"We will spend some time together, honest. Can I take the stories with me?"

She handed him an envelope, giving the smile he was used to seeing on Mio's face. God, he was already attached to Belen, and it seemed she was becoming attached to Evans, too.

Little Primo cried and clung to Mio.

"We'll go to the zoo, to the beach, whatever you want, when we return," Mio promised, translating for Evans. The toddler wouldn't let go. Evans was touched by Mio's love for the child. He was so tender with him and Violeta it took Evans' breath away.

"You've never broken a promise to them yet." Belen kissed her brother's cheeks as she took her son in her arms. "We'll be here waiting."

Outside the house, Mio let out a breath. "It kills me saying goodbye to that boy. You know I was in the delivery room when he was born?"

Evans smiled. "You were?"

"I swear he tumbled right out into my hands. For me . . . it was love at first sight."

"Where was Gilberto?"

Mio's face hardened as he started the car. "I have no idea."

He drove away from the house, turned, and headed back toward the city. "He was there for Violeta's birth, only because I found him, drunk in a bar, and dragged him to the hospital." He reached across the seat for Evans's hand. "I know she wanted babies and she has two beautiful children now, but he is still a crazy man. I must do something about him when we get back."

Evans didn't want to ask what that something might entail. They'd talk about it later.

At the apartment, they ran inside, and before the door even closed, threw off their clothes. Kissing each other, they ran tongues and hands over one another's bodies.

"I dream of your cock, Evans," Mio said, sucking it into his mouth.

Evans had never felt when he was with Mio that he was doing things by rote . . . that he was anything less than impassioned when they were together. Mio looked so hot when he sucked cock and Evans had a sudden urge to watch his lover's porn movies.

He didn't suggest it. He wanted nothing to break the spell of Mio apparently intoxicated by what was between Evans's thighs. Mio licked and sucked . . . he had a thing for the perineum, which Evans had never felt so well treated since he met his sexy Spanish lover. Mio knew all the sensitive places on a man's body. Evans felt his whole body ripple with pleasure when Mio put Evans on his back and began licking his ass hole.

Mio stroked on Evans's cock as he sucked his ass. His whole body trembled. Evans pulled and tweaked at his nipples and came so hard his feet beat down on Mio's sturdy back.

"You're a bull," Mio said, straddling Evans's thighs and entering him fast.

Evans gripped his lover's ass, loving the sounds and smells of two men fucking. He made one fervent wish to the universe. *I want it to always be this way.*

Mio gripped Evans' sensitive cock between the grappling bodies.

"This is mine," Mio rasped in his ear. "Only mine."

"Yes, yes." Evans clutched his lover's ass as Mio came inside him, the force so possessive . . . so frenzied, he almost came again.

They slept, Mio's cock slipping out of Evans but remaining between his ass cheeks. Evans loved they feel of Mio's full body weight on him. He couldn't remember loving anyone this much. He'd never felt so in sync with a man. When Mio stirred, only to shift his thigh under Evans, holding him closer, Evans felt his heart opening wide.

Mio roused himself to pack their things. He was a fastidious organizer, Evans discovered. He packed all the things he knew his client liked him to wear from white boxer briefs, white silk kimonos, and the best Italian suits. He made Evans try everything on that he would be wearing, lending him gossamer-thin shirts that must have been the rage in Portofino. He selected the personal products they would need.

He sniffed Evans' deodorant and rejected it.

"Why?" asked Evans.

"Carlo's wife likes gardenia. She uses everything gardenia so we must, too, so she won't notice anything strange when he goes back to their room."

"God," Evans said. "It's like a military exercise."

He was surprised to see Mio remove a couple of unopened disposable anal douches from a box in the closet.

"I make him use this. I can't stand to eat or fuck a dirty ass," Mio said. "He is not clean, like us."

"Do a lot of guys have dirty asses?" Evans asked, lounging on the bed watching Mio's methodical procedure.

"You've got no idea. That's why I stopped shooting porn. They have the worst asses, some of them. The guys that have been fisted and gang-banged a lot have no idea they leak all over the place. Some of them know it but can't do anything about it. They wear adult diapers, and they are young. It's horrible."

"Sounds like it."

"Which is why you and I will not take some guy's arm up our butts."

Evans shook his head, trying to dispel the image.

Mio grinned. "Baby, you have the cleanest, tightest ass and sweet come. I can't keep my mouth off you."

This struck Evans as terribly funny. He laughed so hard, Mio soon joined him, moving the suitcase aside on the bed to cover his face with kisses.

Mio wrestled himself away, his cock hard again as he resumed his organizing.

"We're taking one suitcase?" Evans asked.

"Yes. I'll carry that and my laptop. You can bring your own laptop and our cabin bag, okay?"

"No problem."

Mio snapped his fingers. "We have to wax you a little."

"You're kidding, right?"

"Do I sound like I'm funny?"

"No."

Mio smiled. "You have good grooming, but not enough for a call boy. I need to get some things ready, so stay naked, guapo."

"Okay." Naked was good. Mio returned with a small dish.

"What's that?"

"Anal bleach."

"What?"

"Come on, *querido,* on your belly, then get up on your knees. It won't burn you. It will feel cool."

Evans was astonished to find his ass hole covered in cool slime.

"I never experienced anything like this."

"This part will sting a little."

Mio put hot wax strips down his ass, rubbed them quickly, then pulled. Evans yelped.

"Sorry." Mio leaned closer. "Missed a spot." He rubbed and pulled again and then moved to the other cheek.

"Ow."

"Mio stroked his burning ass and moved around to kiss him.

"We deserve our money, no?"

Evans gasped, the pain of the waxing still stinging his butt.

Mio took pity on him, opened another container and wiped the bleach off his ass. He then smoothed on some gel that smelled like lavender flowers.

"Turn over."

Mio didn't have much to wax here since Evans liked having a smooth cock and balls, but Mio still did a clean-up job, leaving a tiny tuft of hair at the crotch, following up with the gel. They kissed and sucked each other's mouths, ending up in a heated sixty-nine, only it was asses getting tongued, not cock.

They jerked each other off into near-simultaneous orgasms, swallowing each other's erupting shafts before it was too late.

"Oh, I love you," Mio said, pulling Evans into his arms. They fell asleep and didn't wake up until late in the night.

"Are you hungry?" Mio asked him, kissing his mouth and throat, waking him up.

"No. Only for you."

Mio laughed, his cock hard against Evans's ass.

"We have to wait. We'll have fun in Portofino."

Evans drifted to sleep once again, pleased that Mio wanted him, too. He reached his hand around and cupped his lover's balls.

"You are bad," Mio muttered, laying a gentle bite on the back of Evans's neck. "Bad."

The next morning, they discovered they traveled well together. They both awoke on the first sound of the digital clock radio, kissed each other and showered together, their bodies yearning for sexual relief.

"You keep me hard all the time," Mio said. "No one ever did that to me before."

They dressed in their smart pants and shirts and loafers. Mio had found a pair in his extensive wardrobe that fit Evans. He felt very European and very slutty as Mio ran a possessive hand against Evans's cock.

There was a tap at the front door as they checked for last minute items.

"St. Michel," Mio said as Evans shot him a curious glance. "I booked a car service."

It was still dark outside since it was four o'clock in the morning. They sipped espresso in tiny cups provided by the driver. Mio pulled Evans close, keeping his hand on Evans' thigh. They arrived at the airport in twenty minutes. They checked the suitcase through and headed to the Alitalia First-Class departure lounge after a long wait through customs and security.

As they waited for the flight to board, Evans read the front page of a day-old *New York Times*. America seemed so far away. Mio opened his laptop, checking his stock portfolio. He'd done this when they were together in Miami, and Evans smothered a smile when Mio glanced over at him. Mio seemed pleased with the results.

"Did you check your stock since you arrived?"

Evans felt his stomach muscles contract. His *stock* was Mio's way of bringing up Nora North.

"No." He didn't want to discuss Nora. She was a million miles and lifetimes away.

"Was the visit to the hospital very bad?" Mio asked. It

was the first time they had discussed it since he'd arrived and Evans sure didn't want to talk about it now.

"It was terrible."

Mio held his gaze, his expression unreadable. "We have a nice little trip in the sun. You will forget about her."

Evans laughed. Mio could be a trip all on his own. He handed Evans his iPod.

"I want you to listen to the Italian phrases I recorded for you. Nice little things Carlo likes to hear."

"Is he good-looking?" Evans slipped the earbuds into his ears.

"He's got a nice big cock and clean fingernails. You want another coffee, guapo?"

Guapo nodded and watched half the airport turn to admire the hot swagger of his man as he sauntered over to the uniformed personnel setting up refreshments on a table across the room.

The song "Ti Amo" played on the iPod. It was a sexy love song, for sure. Umberto Tozzi. Evans remembered the less compelling American version recorded by Laura Branigan. He wondered what happened to Umberto Tozzi after all these years. He closed his eyes and wondered why Mio had brought up Nora North. His eyes flew open.

Shit! He's seen something online.

He turned off the iPod and picked up the laptop Mio had left on the seat beside him. Mio was still online. Thank God for wireless. He saw the icon for TMZ miniaturized on the bottom of the screen.

Oh, God. The headline read *Celebwreck Nora North Checks Out Of Rehab.* She looked like a thousand miles of bad road. She had signed on to do *The Surreal Life,* the TV show that put C and D grade celebrities in residence together.

"'My life is taking a turn for the better,'" the tabloid site quoted her as saying. "'No more sycophants. No more hangers-on.'"

Sycophants? Hangers-on? That's all she knows.

She looked deranged in the photo on the TMZ page. He hated TMZ. They got the scoop each and every time and were rarely wrong. Her nose looked awful, and they had taken a close-up picture of it. Underneath it the caption read, *Got Coke?*

He focused on breathing and looked up to see Mio coming back with coffee.

"I'm sorry," Mio said. "Her nose is really bad, no?"

"Really bad."

"Guapo, did she hit you? I swear if this bitch touched you again, I will kill her."

Mio moved into the seat beside him, holding onto the coffees, his fingers turning white he gripped the cups so hard.

"She didn't touch me."

Mio seemed to relax. "Turn it off," he commanded, and Evans shut down the computer. They drew a few curious gazes, but Evans focused on Mio.

"Mio, I don't know why she hates me so much."

"She doesn't hate you, she hates herself." He shifted in his seat. "I ah, worked with a performer once. A long time ago." He sipped his coffee and dropped his voice. "I almost fell for him. He was beautiful and hot, but he had a bad drug problem. He made fun of it. He had an obsession with death. He sat there on a warm, sunny morning in Palm Springs—"

"You shot a movie in Palm Springs?"

Mio frowned. "Yes. Anyway, he was complaining about life and how he wanted to die. I rescued him the next morning. He'd overdosed on a homemade drug called GHB. I called the police because we were all worried when he didn't show up to the set. We were at this big resort, and I climbed up onto the balcony and got into his room. And he was angry! Angry that he was still alive."

"And what happened to him?"

Mio glanced away and let out a small sigh. "He finally

did it. Went to New York two weeks later, booked a hotel room and took drugs and died."

"I'm sorry." Evans touched Mio's hand.

Mio stiffened. "The point is, we can't make people love themselves more than they do. We can't give them the will to live."

"That's true."

"Your stock, ah, you know, she doesn't want to be here. You can't help her, and I won't let her hurt you anymore." He gave Evans an intense look. "I want to protect you. She deals with me now. Okay?"

"Thank you for saying that."

"I mean it."

Evans blinked. He'd never had a partner who cared like Mio did. He didn't like the idea of Nora dying, but the person she was now wasn't one he cared to hang out with. He packed the laptop away and took the coffee from Mio, who threw caution to the wind and kissed him. The heat rose between them.

"I want to fuck you," Mio whispered.

"I think you should."

Mio chuckled. "I think you should listen to the iPod, Everest."

"Why is the song here? Is this one of his favorites?"

"No, Everest. It is how I feel about Evans."

That only made both Evans and Everest want to get down and dirty with Mio.

"You will. Now, listen. Please."

Evans turned his attention to the music again, but Mio nudged him.

"Did you ever meet your birth parents again? You know . . . after the first time in the therapist's office?"

"No. They felt ambushed, and I didn't blame them."

"They don't want to see you again?"

"No, and my parents, my real parents, haven't forgiven me."

"I'm sorry." Mio slipped his arm around him. "I'm very sorry."

"Me, too." Evans closed his eyes, listened to the rest of the song and the lines Mio had recorded for him. He finished his coffee as the flight started to board. He and Mio moved as one to the front of the line since first-class boarded first, after passengers who needed help or had small children.

Evans couldn't wait to take Primo and Violeta on a trip. *Whoa! I'm getting ahead of myself here.* The idea made Evans feel giddy with pleasure.

"Good-looking guys, think they're models?" somebody asked. Evans felt himself standing a little straighter. They took their seats and Mio slipped on an eye mask.

He slept for the entire eighty-five-minute flight as Evans listened once more to the iPod and fought the mental demons struggling with his sense of well-being.

They landed in Rome, and Evans felt a sense of complete ease as they left the gate, the terminal alive with activity and it was just touching nine o'clock. They went through immigration and retrieved their suitcase. Just outside baggage claim, a limo driver held up a sign that read *J.A.*

Mio's chin jutted toward it. "That's us, Everest."

The driver lit up when he saw Mio.

"*Signore* Alejandro!"

"*Buongiorno,* Mario. This is my friend, *Signore* Everest."

Mario was a good-looking, strapping Italian. Wow, if he was anything to go by and he was the hired help, Evans wondered how hot Carlo would be.

The driver led the way outside to a sleek black BMW. He handed them each a champagne kir. They'd had no food, but Mio put on his sunglasses and sipped happily. As the car sped away, Mio reached over and rubbed Evans's cock through his pants.

"Drink," he whispered in his ear. "It's good."

Evans felt light-headed from the champagne and the hand-to-cock resuscitation as they arrived at the port a few minutes later. Marco parked the car, retrieved their belongings from the trunk, and walked quickly to a boat dock.

"He's got a nice ass, no?" Mio asked Evans.

"You fucked him?"

"Hell, no. But I can admire a cute bungalow even though I am about to enjoy the lavish castle."

They stepped onto a large speed boat, and Evans let loose a wild laugh. One day, he'd have a story and a half for Hollywood.

The boat took off across the choppy, foamy, blue-green water. Mio grinned at Evans, their shared exhilaration. The fast ride, the hot sun, the other boats drifting lazily behind them, and the naughtiness of their mission mirrored as their hands entwined for one brief moment. Mario showed off his motor-boating skills, making Mio laugh.

Evans finished his drink as they entered Positano Bay. The hotel glittered like a dazzling, many-faceted jewel ahead of them. Both men stared at the boat slowed at the edge of a tiny pier. Mario spoke into his cell phone and *put-puttered* the boat to the dock. Two uniformed men smiled down at Evans and Mio.

"Welcome to the edge of heaven, baby," Mio said and gulped down the last of his champagne.

CHAPTER SEVEN

The hotel workers scurried to take their bags up to the hotel, but Evans matched Mio's assured, leisurely pace as he paused to smell the flowers growing in the lush gardens lining the path. The feeling of decadent, sun-soaked splendor was offset by stark white walls, some of which were covered with ivy. Imaginative, opulent fresh flower displays, thick Persian carpets, fabulous artwork, and gigantic crescent-shaped white sofas seemed designed for pure sensual enjoyment. As they approached the front desk, Evans tried hard to act nonchalant, but the elegant yet homey furnishings made this hotel the kind of place you felt was almost too beautiful and too good to be true.

Mio took the lead, checking them into their room.

The concierge smiled, welcoming them and handed them a tasseled key card envelope. "You have one of our special rooms, number eleven. It has an extra large patio." When the man noticed Evans staring out at the huge terraces, he beamed.

"Each terrace overlooks the ocean from different angles. We can bring you coffee, or something cold to drink. Please feel free to look around."

As Evans fell into step with Mio, they passed a group of men, the first of them, a well-built, powerful-looking man with jet black hair slicked back from his forehead. Though no looks were exchanged and there was absolutely no sign of recognition from either man, Evans, long-schooled in the art of gaydar, felt certain this was Carlo Bercovici. Something primal echoed between him and Mio. It was subtle but strong enough to make Evans feel damp behind the ears and in his pants.

They arrived at their room.

Mio pressed some folded notes into the bellboy's hand. Once they were alone, Evans had to know.

"Was that him?"

Mio seemed surprised. "You read body language well. Yes, that was him." He ran a practiced glance around the room. "Could be bigger, but the patio is fantastic."

He wasn't wrong. Evans was surprised the room was small but elegant. A huge bed dominated it, a small coffee table, love seat and a couple of chairs opposite it.

They stood outside, and Mio pointed out his favorite spots—the bay of Salerno and the coast of Capri in the distance.

His fingers traced colorful tiles on a stone bench overlooking the ocean. "This tile work here is all from the seventeenth century."

Evans pressed his body into Mio's. "I'm so excited and so nervous and—"

Mio kissed him, squeezing his ass. "*Querido,* we must get ready. Did you see what's on the coffee table?"

Evans turned to look. A bucket with champagne chilling on ice and a lot of red roses.

"Did you order those?"

Mio nodded. "I took you away from Barcelona, the city of love. I promise you, no matter what happens, we'll be there for La Díada de Sant Jordi. In the meantime, you must have roses."

"What happens on La Díada de Sant Jordi?"

Mio slipped Evans's jacket and shirt from his body. "You'll see. We exchange gifts."

"Roses?"

Mio grinned. "And a book. Listen, I'm not going to talk about love when we're here to fuck."

Evans laughed. "How come I am the only one naked?"

Mio pretended to be affronted. "Because you haven't undressed me yet."

Evans took off Mio's clothes. Before he could rub himself up against his lover, Mio put their suits and shirts on hangers and threw open the suitcase.

"Come on, guapo. We make ourselves super-sexy now."

"I don't think you could be any sexier, Mio."

"Thank you. Come on."

In the bathroom, which stopped Evans cold it was so spectacular, Mio left the douche by the bidet for Carlo to use. They showered together under a tepid spray, ogling their floor-to-ceiling view of the Amalfi coastline. Mio soaped Evans with gardenia shower gel and, just as he was enjoying the sensation of having his back and ass squeezed and rubbed, Mio's voice cut into his pleasure.

"My turn, baby."

Evans returned the favor and, just as he was enjoying his fingers creeping up Mio's ass crack, his lover turned off the taps.

He reached for towels. "Be quick now. Leave your skin a little moist."

Evans did as he was told. Mio opened a small bottle and squirted some oil onto his hands. He rubbed it over Evans's body, paying special attention to his abs, cock, balls, and finally his ass.

Once again, Evans repeated this ritual for Mio, who then handed him a pair of white boxer briefs that left nothing to the imagination. Mio put on his own pair, and they studied themselves in the bathroom mirror.

"I can't believe this is me." Evans admired his own manly image. His abs looked tipped, his arm and thigh muscles defined.

Mio broke the spell. "One thing missing." He took a length of rubber from the toiletry bag and out on the balcony, held the rubber to the ground, stepping on it. He gripped the ends with his hands doing a quick workout, every muscle in his body straining with the effort.

"You do it now," he told Evans. "I want your muscles to pop."

Evans did as he was told.

"Stand up." Mio ran his hands over Evans's body. "Nice."

Evans's arms shook from the effort of working the tight hose.

Mio barely had time to throw the hose back into their suitcase when there was a knock at the door.

Evans's heart began to race.

"This is it," Mio said, a sly smile curving the corners of his beautiful mouth. "It will go better if you think of me as Alejandro."

He dropped a quick kiss on Evans's mouth. The truth was he was more excited now than nervous. He felt like he was a character in the old TV series *Queer as Folk*. They strode in unison to the door. Mio looked like a Greek sea god come to life, his brown skin glistening good health. His thick, huge cock accentuated by the tight white briefs made Evans long for him. Mio glanced down at Evans's crotch and ran his fingers across his cock. Evans found himself responding, and by the time Mio opened the door, Carlo stood there, eyes popping as he saw the two hot, hung men waiting for him.

"*Mi amore*," Mio said, and stood back, allowing the handsome Italian entry.

The endearment threw Evans, but he kept a smile on his face. Carlo eyed Evans, but his lust was all for Mio.

"I missed you, Alejandro."

Mio smiled. "I missed you, too." He kissed Carlo's cheeks

Continental-style and ran his hand down Carlo's back, introducing Everest. "He's a new model I am working with."

"Nice. Very nice." Carlo could hardly contain himself. His hand went from Evans's crotch, straight to Mio's hard cock straining against the stretched briefs. He pulled out the juicy cock waiting for his attention, Mio's cock and balls squishing down the fabric and looking even bigger than they had that morning.

"I don't think I can wait," Carlo said.

All three men went outside to the sunny, stone-floored patio. Evans waited for Mio's lead. Mio laughed as Carlo popped the champagne and poured three glasses. He picked up a glass, kicked off his leather loafers, and bent to suck Mio's cockhead. Evans wasn't jealous.

He was shocked to discover he was even more turned on and ready to fuck any time Mio gave him the word.

Mio took a glass and handed it to Evans, snatching up the last one as Carlo, his hand deep in Mio's burrowed underpants, toasted them both.

"Thank you both for coming here. *Salut.*"

Carlo sat beside Mio on a stone bench. He lifted Mio off the bench for a moment, pulling down the briefs and licking across his rippled torso and down his body.

Mio made a face of concentrated bliss. Evans's view from a chair opposite them was obscured.

He caught a glimpse as Carlo knelt between Mio's thighs, saw the rampant hunger as he licked and sucked Mio's balls, tugging on them with his lips. Mio pursed his lips. It was a gesture he never made when he was with Evans. Evans watched, fascinated.

"I need you," Carlo said.

Mio's eyes opened. He lowered his legs to the ground, his cock flying high, and took Carlo's hand in his.

"Give us ten minutes, okay?"

Evans nodded. He watched Carlo manhandling Mio, his hand down the back of Mio's briefs. The two men went into the bedroom. Evans could see easily into it since there were only white sheers billowing against a faint breeze. The two men disappeared into the bathroom.

Evans could hear them laughing, heard the word *douche* and fought the rumble of hunger in his belly. He looked away when they came out naked and heard them laughing together, the whispered endearments.

The sex started fast. Of course, he remembered, Carlo didn't like kissing. Evans felt ridiculously pleased about that. Kissing would have made it too intimate. He focused on breathing and glanced back at the bed. It was hard to watch Mio eating the guy's ass like it was his last supper.

"Oh fuck, oh yeah . . . oh, Alejandro . . ." Carlo kept up a litany as he lay on his back, Mio kneeling between his thighs, opening his legs up wider, his mouth glued to the Italian man's ass. He had a nice big cock. Mio hadn't been lying.

"Eat me, oh . . . lick me." Man, he was in heaven in the bedroom.

Evans watched Mio's hard cock nudge at Carlo's ass hole. He rubbed and poked and got the head in and went right back to feasting on him again. Evans started getting hot now. It was sexy as hell watching the scene before him.

Carlo was beckoning him. "Join us, Everest. Come taste my cock."

Evans stood and walked to the bed. Mio never glanced up from the ass he was sucking with such passion.

"Take them off." Carlo's fingers plucked at the briefs.

Evans slipped them down, and Carlo grabbed his cock with both hands and sucked. Evans tried not to react to the teeth grazing him. The guy lacked real ability but had tons of enthusiasm.

He knelt by the bed and sucked Carlo's cock into his

mouth. His pre-come tasted salty, which surprised him. He worked on the cock which kept slickening under his touch and finally, Mio pushed him away.

"Oh yeah, fuck my ass," Carlo whispered.

Evans stood by and watched his lover dominate the man on the bed. He took him hard, with deliberate, plodding, heavy strokes. Carlo writhed. His mouth fell open and, as Mio quickened his pace, he lowered his body onto Carlo, who grabbed his ass cheeks.

Mio was coming. Evens could tell.

Carlo gasped, his hot white come coating his torso and running down his thigh as Mio lifted himself away and plunged back down again.

"Clean him up for me," Mio said, rolling off Carlo.

Evans got between Carlo's thighs and licked the come from his sweaty body. He was surprised how good it felt. He was even more surprised when Mio moved behind Evans and licked his ass. Carlo's cock needed a break. It lay against his thigh. Through heavy-lidded eyes, he gazed at them.

"Suck each other's cocks for me."

Mio and Evans moved into a sixty-nine beside him. Carlo touched them in turn, his fingers dipping into their ass cracks, his tongue lapping at them.

"I love the way you smell," he said.

Evans' spirit seemed to somersault, and the scent of gardenia intensified with the mingled body heat. At one point Carlo nudged Evans away and slurped on Mio's hard cock. As soon as he moved away, Evans resumed his cock-sucking duties.

Mio's hands shot to Evans's head, his thumbs caressing the base of his skull. Evans wanted to eat the man up he was so hot.

The sounds of sucking and fucking got to Evans. A faint breeze and the tang of ocean air revived him in the tangle of fire on the bed. Mio sat up and positioned Evans on his cock, facing him. Evans lowered himself onto Mio's cock, aware of Carlo's hand gripping Mio's cock beneath him. He raised himself up and felt Carlo's fingers running up the shaft.

"Take it all, take him in your ass," Carlo rasped, removing his hand.

Evans ground down on his lover's cock. He wrapped his legs around Mio's waist. Mio held him, fucking him. His cock felt huge. Evans came, Carlo's hand curled around the head.

"Fuck me, fuck me. It's my turn," Carlo chanted, and Evans climbed off Mio as his cock was still erupting. Carlo had a tight ass, and Evans sought for entry. He turned Carlo around, away from him and the Italian moaned with delight.

"God . . . your cock . . . it is the best."

He gripped the base of his own cock as Mio shot into him with a cry. Mio bucked underneath Carlo who rotated his hips down, the way Evans knew Mio liked him to do when he was riding him this way.

"You ready?" he asked. Mio's eyes were black with his desire. He lifted himself off Mio's moist cock, stroking himself.

"I'm going to fuck you like no man ever took you, whore."

Mio came out of his come-high and grinned, rolling over on his belly. Carlo pulled him up, slicing into Mio. Mio's leg muscles rippled as he pushed back against the man riding him.

Evans felt he was watching something private and primal and, for the first time, remembered this was his lover being taken so aggressively.

Carlo fucked Mio, and Mio seemed to enjoy the cock dance. He matched Carlo's rhythmic pounding, his gaze meeting Evans's intense one. Mio smiled at him.

"Oh, hot ass," Carlo shouted and came hard, pushing Mio's upper body down on the bed.

He stroked himself off in Mio's ass, finally removing himself and slapping Mio's butt cheek as he pushed himself away.

"You have the afternoon and evening free," he said as Mio stayed down on the bed, twisting himself around to gaze up at Carlo.

"I'm sorry I had to bring my wife with me, but I'll come when she's asleep."

"Beautiful," Mio said.

Carlo gave Mio's cock a little squeeze and went into the bathroom. They heard the shower running. Mio lay still, an arm across his brow.

Evans sat beside him. "Are you okay?"

"Yes."

Evans knew Mio didn't want to be touched. He sensed it. They didn't say anything else until Carlo emerged, fully dressed.

"How do I look?" he asked.

"Like I could fuck you all over again," Mio said.

"You will." Carlo gave an unruly strand of hair a swipe as it fell out of his eyes.

He left the room, closing the door softly. Evans watched Mio spring up the second the door was closed.

"Put the do not disturb sign on it, will you?" Mio asked and went into the bathroom. Evans did as he was asked and heard the shower running. No, the bidet. He heard the shower after that and realized Mio had been tense. When he emerged, he was the Mio he knew and loved.

"Your turn," Mio said.

Evans didn't need to be told twice. He raced to the shower, toweled off,\ and returned to the room where Mio paced the floor.

"Guapo, let's take a little drive into town. We need to eat now." He called the front desk, asking for the Mercedes service.

They dressed quickly and headed back to the front desk where a driver awaited them.

"We'd like to have some lunch," Mio said. "Do they still have the great scampi at Da u Batti?"

The driver nodded. "It's very good, sir."

They climbed in back of the sleek black car; Mio grasped Evans's hand for a brief moment. They passed colorful shops and houses painted in bright, burnt orange, pale yellows, blues, and even olive greens. It was like Brigadoon and Evans sat glued to the window. Mio reached out a hand at one point and squeezed his thigh. Brightly-painted roofs and doors bursting with plant life embedded in window boxes across the frames were a wonderful, fairy-tale touch. The tropical feel soothed the senses. Beautiful, chic women hurried past with boutique bags. European men dressed in the same manner as Mio and Evans walked quickly, everyone with a cell phone to the ear.

As the car drove onto a small street in the pretty center of Positano, Mio said, "This is the best restaurant in town. I can't wait for you to try it."

Mio tipped the driver. "Can you come back for us in two hours?"

"Certainly, sir."

Mio put his hand at the small of Evans's back as they took some stairs up to a cobblestoned piazza. The restaurant itself was squeezed between two houses. A huge pair of anchors, covered in barnacles loomed over the entrance. Evans immediately liked the nautical theme. The wonderful artwork on the walls had marine themes, but Mio was too busy looking for the best table. The restaurant was filling up fast. He pointed to the one he wanted. They were very small tables, but Evans loved it, since he was with the man he adored.

Their table overlooked the street, the pale orange tablecloth matching the paint colors of the closest buildings.

"Wow, it's so romantic, Mio." Evans loved seeing the tiny staircases lining the houses and shops, some of which were on stilts. Mio's hand groped for Evans's and the tablecloths made for a convenient place to hide their now entwined hands.

"This restaurant specializes in seafood," Mio said. "What would you like, guapo?"

"I'd like for you to never let go of my hand and to order for us."

Mio smiled. "I like your ideas. We must have the scampi. Oh, they have pasta." He turned in his seat, engaging their lively waiter in fluent Italian. There was no printed menu, but Mio seemed to know their selections well and picked out dishes like pesto and clams.

"Would you like to try some grappa?" Mio asked Evans.

He nodded, eager for this new adventure. The waiter quickly returned with a bottle and two shot glasses. Evans was surprised when Mio remove his hand from his own, dipping his index finger into the first poured shot. He rubbed it on the back of his hand and sniffed.

"Excellent," he said, and the waiter poured a second glass for Evans.

"What was that?" Evans asked.

"It's the only way to taste it, by smell. You have to be able to smell the grapes. See?" Mio held his hand over to Evans who licked it instead of sniffing it.

Mio shook his head and laughed. "Guapo, you keep me hard, always."

"You're hard?"

Mio's hand sought Evans's under the cloth again. "Yes, and if you touch me to check we'll wind up in jail for having public sex."

"Really? How cute are the local cops?"

Mio laughed. The waiter returned with two plates of scampi, which unlike scampi Evans had eaten in California, turned out to be lobster.

The waiter explained American-Italian cuisine was different to true, authentic Italian cooking. "Scampi here means the sauce, which is white wine, butter, and garlic. We serve lobster here because it is our specialty. We can serve it with shrimp, but here, we like lobster."

So did Evans. The dish was rich, buttery and loaded with garlic.

"It won't matter," Mio insisted. "We're only kissing each other."

"But what about Carlo?"

"He never likes to kiss, remember?"

"I can't keep my mouth off you," Evans said.

"As soon as we're back in our room, I'd like proof of that, please," Mio said as a second dish of fragrant shrimp and rice arrived. Mio refilled their glasses. The grappa was strong, spicy and worked its rustic charm on Evans. He forked a piece of fish grilled with bay leaves and lime and was pretty certain they'd left the edge of heaven and found their way deep inside it.

"Limoncello?" Mio asked him when every last bite of food was gone.

Evans nodded, feeling quite drunk with happiness. All his senses responded to the magic of the tiny town, and he felt Mio draw nearer.

"Only one," Mio said. "Then we have a siesta."

They kissed and licked each other's faces and bodies for an hour in their room overlooking the sea. Mio sucked Evans's cock. "You taste of grappa, guapo," he said, and for some reason they thought this was hilarious and fell on the floor, laughing.

Mio wrapped himself around Evans, dragging the top sheet off the bed. They dozed on and off, the sound of boats and people occasionally waking them. It was late afternoon when Evans awoke with a hard cock seeking entry inside him. He turned back and was shocked to see it was Carlo.

"What the . . ."

He blinked. Not Carlo. It was Mio, but it was a weird moment.

"What's wrong?" Mio asked. "You want to sleep more?"

"No, no." Evans pulled Mio's arm around him tighter.

"You're shaking," Mio said, putting warm kisses on his neck and shoulder.

"I had the weirdest feeling you were Carlo."

Mio grinned. "You disappointed?"

"Oh, my God . . . Mio. No."

"Show me then." Evans turned and kissed Mio, whose own kisses grew more feverish. Mio put Evans on his back on the floor and fucked him with a slow rocking motion Evans had come to dream of, increasing his pace as they both came close to coming. Evans felt his lover's warm and natural rhythm as he met each thrust.

They came together, Mio leaning down and kissing him.

When they caught their breath again, Mio bit Evans's chin playfully. "Want to go to the beach?"

"Sure."

They grabbed their swimsuits and towels. They left their room and walked across the hotel floor to a different elevator.

"This elevator is built right into the mountain and comes out at the beach," Mio told him. "It's for guests only."

As they walked down the path to the soft, golden sand, they saw a family of a mother, father, and two chattering children coming back from the ocean. The parents were draped over one another, kissing and laughing. Evans was stunned to see it was Carlo.

Boy, you never can tell. You'd never know he'd been up in our bed begging Mio to fuck him.

There was no sign of recognition or acknowledgement on either side, but as soon as they passed, Evans glanced at Mio. He'd been taken by surprise, too.

"*Sono omosessuale?*" the boy asked his mother who shushed him.

Carlo, however, said, "*Sí,*" and laughed. "*Penso tani.*"

The family passed them. Mio glanced at Evans, his brow cocked.

"He only *thinks* we're gay? Tonight we show his Italian ass just how gay we are."

CHAPTER EIGHT

As wonderful as Portofino was, Evans was happy to return to Barcelona. Carlo had returned to their room for a quickie around three in the morning. Mio fucked him from behind, Carlo surprising them both by sucking off Evans.

"I want to see you both again," he'd said, hugging them both and slipping back to his room.

At dawn, Mio and Evans packed.

"I don't want to leave my roses," he said to Mio. "I wish I could take them with me."

"Guapo . . . I will give you roses at home every day."

"But these are so beautiful, Mio."

"We'll pack a few in the suitcase." Mio wrapped them in plastic, putting them on top of their clothing. "Evans, you are so sweet, my man."

They left the hotel.

"I am so glad to go home," Mio said. "I feel Primo calling us."

As soon as they touched down in Barcelona, Mio called his sister, who told him she and the children were waiting for them. A hired car waited for them, and they sank into the luxurious seat, kissing on the way home.

"Oh, look." Evans broke off the kiss as they approached Las Ramblas. "Mio, look at all the roses!"

Mio laughed. "I buy you some."

Evans shook his head. "No, I want the ones in our suitcase."

Mio took Evans's face in his hands and kissed him deeper.

114

When they arrived home and opened the suitcase, how-ever, the roses were gone, along with a couple of Mio's ex-pensive Italian shirts.

"Airport baggage thieves," he griped, but he didn't seem really upset. They showered together, slipping on jeans and tennis shoes.

They drove to Mio's family home, passing by his father's shop. Two old men sat outside playing cards. One was his father who smiled and waved. Mio and Evans waved back.

How weird, one day he looks angry, the next day he's waving and smiling.

At the house, little Primo clattered down the stairs, drag-ging a toy wagon with him, showing it off to them.

Mio held the little boy, kissing his cheeks. Primo clung to him, letting Evans kiss a small spot on his forehead.

"What a character," Evans said, rubbing the child's back.

"Isn't he?" Mio asked.

Evans took the wagon back into the house, Mio carrying his nephew.

His mom ran to them from the stove where she was stuff-ing a chicken. A long discussion ensued about lunch being ready soon.

Primo ran around the house with his wagon, and the con-versation seemed to take a dark turn.

"She needs some lemons. Do you mind going to my dad's store and getting some?" Mio asked Evans.

"Is everything okay?"

Mio nodded, but Evans had the distinct feeling he was be-ing asked to make himself scarce, especially since there was a huge basket of lemons on the kitchen windowsill. He agreed, however, and walked to the front door.

As he suspected, the discussion—or what really sounded like a heated argument—ensued as soon as they thought he was gone. He heard the name Gilberto. Belen's ex-husband. Evans wondered what he'd done this time.

He walked down the hill to the small shop he realized now was called Casa Cortez. The name was emblazoned above a horseshoe nailed over the entrance. His eyes adjusted to the light as he entered. Mio's dad stood at the counter reading a newspaper. He held an espresso cup aloft, eyeing Evans as if assessing his potential for violence.

"*Hola*," Evans said.

Mio's dad nodded but showed no sign of remembering him or even wanting to remember him. The man's gaze dropped back to his paper and back to Evans again. He sipped his coffee. Evans felt very awkward now. He felt he was interrupting Mio's dad in a private moment. He backed away, looking around the store, surprised to see how well-stocked it was. He hadn't been sure what to expect. He certainly hadn't expected such a Cosmopolitan place with newspapers from different European countries on a rack. Each newspaper was secured by a wooden pole. He hadn't seen these for years and loved this invention. You could hold the pole, read a full-size paper easily and best of all, turn the pages without getting ink on your fingers.

He scoured the fruit and vegetables and picked up some lemons. There were toys on the shelves, but he resisted buying anything for Primo. He returned to the counter and put the lemons on it.

Evans held up some euros, indicating he wanted to pay for the lemons and then pointed at Señor Cortez's cup.

"Can I buy . . . *una taza de cafe?*" he asked.

Mio's dad scowled. "No!" He put his cup into a sink behind him and went through a set of French doors to a back room. Television. Evans strained to hear if Señor Cortez might be coming back. He scratched his head. Damn. How weird.

He left the lemons on the counter and walked outside. What a strange day this was turning out to be. He wasn't sure if he should go back to the house and decided to give it a few more minutes. He looked longingly over his shoulder at the newspaper rack in the store with the two small coffee tables arranged around it.

He would have loved to sit down and have a coffee, but Mio's dad . . . wow . . . Evans realized he hadn't spoken to Michael. He'd tried to call him twice in Portofino and had no luck. He tried again and became concerned when he reached his voice mail once more. Michael was the kind of guy whose ear had to be surgically removed from his cell phone. He left a message asking for a call back and then called his housekeeper, Stella, too. Hopefully, she was keeping an eye on his house. She didn't pick up either, so he left her a message too.

"Ay-vun?"

It took Evans a moment to realize the male voice behind him meant him. He turned and found Mio's dad grinning at him.

"*Venido*, come," the older man said, suddenly nice again. *What the fuck, the old geezer must be doing happy pills at the back of the shop.*

Mio's dad bustled to the counter. "*¿Cafe?*"

"*Sí, cafe por favor.*"

"*Por nada.*"

Evans watched the old man wield the espresso machine with great showmanship. He kept his eye on him in case the old guy spat in his coffee. When at last it came spurting out of the machine, the old man filled Evans's cup to the brim. He waved away any thought of money. Evans held up the lemons and held out euros.

The old man shook his head and pointed to his mouth, "Not sweet."

"I know." *How did he say for your wife?*

The older man gestured to him and led him through the French doors. Evans was surprised to find they were in a whole other world here. Señor Cortez was loaded with stock of every imaginable can and packaged goods. But he also had books, newspapers, magazines, DVDs, a TV, and a table with two tropical-looking chairs.

He pointed to one and Evans sat.

"No, no." He wagged his finger and pointed to the other one. Evans moved.

Señor Cortez shuffled off, and Evans sipped his coffee, beginning to relax. Perhaps he could win over Mio's dad after all. Less than a minute later, Señor Cortez was back. He stood, hands on hips, glaring at Evans.

"*¡Hacia fuera!*" he shrieked.

Evans knew enough Spanish . . . and the waving of arms to understand he was being told to get out. It shocked him. Hot coffee spilled over his fingers in his haste to leave. He picked up his lemons and the older man went berserk.

He grabbed his phone. Evans heard the words *loco* and *policia*.

Evans pictured an international incident over a cup of coffee and some lemons and quickly left the store, calling Mio on his cell phone. He almost screamed when he got voice mail.

"Mio, I think I'm in trouble," he yelled into the phone. He glanced over his shoulder as he hurried up the hill. Señor Cortez was peering around the entrance to the store, shaking a fist at him.

Oh, my God.

His cell phone rang. Mio. Evans answered and repeated his frightened words. "I'm in trouble. Your father hates me."

"What do you mean trouble?" Mio asked.

Some troubled memory . . . the distant past. It flew back to him now. As a five-year-old, Evans had stolen a foil-wrapped chocolate heart from a local shop. He'd been so guilt-ridden that for the entire day, each time he heard a police siren, he'd been convinced they were coming to arrest him. His mother, when he finally confessed his sin, dragged him to the store and made him apologize. He'd tearfully paid the storekeeper the two cents for the chocolate heart and had to endure the man's eternal mistrust until his family moved to another town.

His ears strained for sirens, and suddenly Mio was coming toward him, a hint of menace in his gait.

"Guapo, what's wrong?"

"I . . . I tried to pay for the lemons, but he wouldn't let me, and then he called the police!"

Mio held him tight in his arms, kissing him. "It's okay. We have some lunch . . . a little siesta. Why did you buy lemons anyway?"

"Because you told me to."

"I did?" Mio frowned as they walked back to the family house. He kept his arm around Evans, who enjoyed the feeling of contained danger emanating from his lover. He felt that Mio would have sprung into physical action and defended him. It made him feel good to know that.

Inside the house, Mio closed the door. "There is a problem with my sister. I will explain later. First, we eat, okay?"

Evans nodded. He felt the urge to burst into tears. All over a two-cent heart.

In the living room, Evans stared at the head of the table. "What the . . . how did he get here so fast?"

"Who?" Mio asked.

"Your father. He was just calling the police."

Mio stared at him for a moment and began to laugh. "Oh, Evans." He doubled over in merriment.

"Papa . . ." Mio shot off rapid-fire Spanish to his father.

Evans was pissed. What was so funny?

Mio's mom and dad laughed. Little Primo took the adults' distraction as an opportunity to grab a cream puff from a platter on the table.

"Baby," Mio said finally, wiping tears of laughter from his eyes. "They're twins."

"Twins?"

"Yeah, my dad and his brother. Now, my dad is called Enzo . . . you should call him that so you know the difference. His brother is Aldo."

"But they are identical," Evans wailed. "How am I supposed to tell them apart?"

"My dad has straight teeth on the bottom. Aldo's mouth looks like a bomb exploded inside it. Now sit guapo, my mother made us paella."

All through lunch, Mio's dad kept pointing a fork at Evans, laughing. Evans grew tired of the joke but tried to shake the bad vibe. He just couldn't help feeling something was wrong, and it had nothing to do with police sirens.

Mio, however, was wonderful, touching Evans's leg under the table, rubbing his back when they were unobserved. As soon as the meal finished, Evans wanted more than anything to be alone with Mio. They exchanged glances and Mio understood, Evans was certain of it. His mom refused to let them help her with the dishes, and Primo raced off to play with the toy wagon, leaving the two men with a little time on their hands.

They went to the room Evans had been given the day he arrived. So much had happened in that short time. It had been only three days, but it felt like months.

Mio pushed the chair up against the door handle, and Evans pushed Mio to the bed.

He unbuckled his lover's belt, unfastened the buttons on his jeans, and his tongue tip reached out for Mio's huge cock.

Mio stroked his head. "Get up here, baby."

Nothing doing. Evans wanted to suck Mio's cock, and he knew that half the pleasure for a man receiving head was being able to look down and watch his lover pleasuring him.

Mio was no exception. He raised himself on his elbows, his hard cock finding a welcome resting place against Evans's flattened tongue.

Evans removed Mio's tennis shoes, massaging his bare feet as he worked over Mio's cock like a pro . . . a pro who loved what he was doing. His fingers sought out Mio's balls. Mio moaned, raising his lips just a little to help ease down his jeans and underpants.

"God, suck me," Mio rasped, stroking the hair back from Evans's face. "Oh, baby . . . that's beautiful."

Evans encircled Mio's huge balls with his fists, squeezing just a little. Mio's feet came off the floor. His cockhead expanded in Evans's mouth. Evans pressed his tongue against the veins protruding from Mio's cock and sucked.

With a shout, Mio came, flooding Evans's throat. Evans was surprised how much come his lover produced and fought to keep Mio's cock in his mouth as Mio bucked and jumped all over the place.

"Fuck, baby, that was hot!" Mio reached down and grabbed Evans. He shucked off Evans's shoes and pulled his lover toward him.

"A little sleep and then, it's your turn." Mio was gone, just like that, his cock still hard against Evans's hand and thigh, his muscular arms keeping Evans hard against his body.

Evans smiled to himself. *Rode hard and put away wet. Just how I like him.* He tried hard not to think about other men bringing Mio such bliss. He closed his eyes, trying not to worry about Michael, the police . . . or chocolate hearts.

The two men were woken by the sounds of yelling in the hallway. Mio pulled himself away from Evans, tucking himself back into his underpants and jeans. He slid his feet into the wrong shoes, then found the right ones, tossing the chair aside. Out in the hallway, Belen and her mother were shouting at each other.

Next thing Evans knew, Mio had joined in the yelling. Poor Belen, her mother, and brother were ganging up on her. Primo stood in the hallway, naked except for pull-ups, crying, the baby squalling in her portable crib.

"Mio," Evans said, picking up Primo. "What's going on?"

"Take the children into the garden," Mio said, his eyes flashing.

Evans put his free arm around Belen. She latched onto him, sobbing into his neck.

"Go," Mio said. "Please."

Evans picked up the baby carrier. It was heavy holding both the toddler and the carrier, and he wondered how Belen did this all the time.

He found the wagon in the kitchen and put Primo into it. The little boy screamed, hard tears falling down his face.

"Come on, Primo, let's go play outside." It was easier dragging the wagon in one hand by the handle and carrying the baby in her carrier. Evans remembered she liked to be swung and tried swaying her back and forth. In the backyard, he spotted the swing Belen had brought to Mio's place and put the baby in it. She became hysterical. He put her in the wagon with Primo. The boy looked down at the screaming bundle between his legs.

"You hold her now; you are her big brother," Evans said, not sure if Primo understood. He pulled the children along, little Primo's sobs continuing, but Evans was pleased to see the child's arms move firmly around his sister. He took them along the stone path, and a yellow daisy hit Primo in the face. He looked up at Evans, surprised. Then he began to laugh.

Laughter. *Good. That's a good sign.* He pretended he was a pony and began to canter and trot. Primo laughed and laughed, loving it when he reached out and ran his hands through the thriving scented blossoms in his grandmother's garden.

A ladybug fell on Evans's hand. He reached down to show Primo who leaned forward to watch as the ladybug's little wings opened up and she flew to a red carnation.

Primo laughed and laughed. Little Violeta lay sideways, and Evans bent down to straighten her. She wasn't laughing, but at least she had stopped crying. Footsteps. Evans looked up, and his heart pumped wildly in his chest. Mio.

"Guapo, I'm sorry." Mio ran to him and hugged him. "You have the magic touch with all the Cortez men, don't you?"

"Except your uncle."

Mio flashed a grin. "Eh . . . he knows now that you're with me. He won't send you to prison for his lemons."

Mio knelt beside Primo and stroked the little boy's head. He watched the way Primo held his sister. "I wish one day we could have the babies . . ." He looked up at Evans, his expression wistful.

"Well, we can enjoy these two, you know."

Mio smiled. "Yes, we can. We promised Primo an outing. We can leave Violeta here with my mother."

As they took Primo inside to dress him for the car ride, a sullen Belen took possession of the baby. Her hooded, hurt glance at her brother tore at Evans. She wouldn't make eye contact with him but insisted on dressing Primo herself.

"I'll give you a bag of things he needs," she said.

Out in the hallway, they waited. Evans couldn't stand it anymore.

"What's going on?"

"She went behind my back to see her husband."

Evans thought for a moment. "Is that a very bad thing? I mean—"

"He is a bad man. He takes drugs. He won't work. She

left him." He cut the air with a karate chop, his voice rising. "That is it."

Evans kept his voice low, aware that Belen might be able to hear them. "But, Mio, they're married. She loves him."

"When it's over, it's over. She went back and had sex with him."

"I agree, that's probably not the wisest step. Counseling and—"

"It's over. When it's over, it's over."

"Mio, I'm surprised at you. He's the father of her children. It will never be over."

"When it's over for me, Evans, it is over."

Evans was surprised at the vehemence in his lover's tone. "I'm on your side, and Belen's . . . but don't you see? They have two very small children. She can't just walk away."

Mio's eyes narrowed. "She needs to be strong."

Oh, boy. "Mio, I'm sorry. I think she needs your support. No wonder she's sneaking around behind your back."

Mio stared at him. Evans felt he'd gone too far and quickly apologized. "She's your sister. I'm sorry. I don't know enough about the situation—"

"No, you don't."

"I'm sorry," Evans said again, feeling wretched.

Belen came out of the room with Primo dressed and ready. It was clear she'd been crying. Primo wrestled his way between the adult legs and jumped for the front door handle.

"You want to come with us?" Evans asked her.

Belen glanced at her brother.

"Come on," Mio said, hugging her. "We go have some fun."

Mio's mother came out and kissed them all goodbye. The house was quiet.

"Enzo has the siesta," she told Evans, pinching his cheeks.

Violeta squalled in the bedroom, and she went running.

"Come on," Mio said. "Let's go. I have something special planned."

Mio wasn't kidding. He drove them to the Plaza de Catalunya train station where they stood in line for the Tramvia Blau. A small blue tram, it appeared to be, judging by the hordes of people waiting to board it, one of the most popular things for families to do in Barcelona. As they crammed into seats together, Evans was surprised how many people could fit inside.

The tram driver made jokes, pointing out actual points of interest, plus some very silly ones. He gestured to a man out on the sidewalk. His comment made everyone laugh.

Evans craned to glimpse the man and was anxious to know what was funny since he didn't understand what the driver said. He asked Mio.

"He said, 'How nice, he is picking his nose.'"

Primo balanced on his mother's knee, shrieking with excitement. Other children chattered noisily, too, as they passed stores, houses, elegant neighborhoods and then into a different, softer world of the mountain. Belen told Evans she and Mio had been going to Tibidabo since they were children.

"What's Tibidabo?"

"An amusement park." Her eyes cleared and she beamed as the tram chugged halfway up a mountain. Everyone on the tram applauded, and Mio took hold of Primo as they disembarked. "We take a little blue train up the mountain now," Mio told Evans.

It seemed a sacred, beloved ritual for brother and sister, who were the best of friends again by the time they reached the top of the mountain via a charming little funicular that took them through wonderful, verdant forests, the smell thoroughly intoxicating. A roar of screams and laughter greeted them at the top of the summit. And there it was. Tibidabo Amusement Park.

Mio took the time to let Evans look at the view of Barcelona. It was a spectacular sight. He asked Primo if he could see the family house. He thought he could, and Evans found himself charmed all over again by the sweet little boy when he said, "I think I see Violeta."

The park itself was fun. It had been built in 1889, according to Mio, and the rides dated back that far. Evans was entranced by the dreamy quality of the place. Most of attendants wore costumes and, after paying the entrance fee, Mio insisted they ride the Ferris wheel. At the very top, he told Primo to close his eyes. Perhaps anticipating some candy, the little boy did as he was told, holding out his hand, but in fact, Mio wanted to kiss Evans. A few seconds later, Primo's eyes flew open.

He seemed shocked to find himself empty-handed.

Back on the ground again, Primo dragged Evans to a roller coaster of quaint little sports cars. Evans had never seen anything like it. It puttered along, making it safe for small riders. Primo reached his little hand out as they rounded the first curve, flipping off people on the ground. His mother grabbed his hand, but Mio laughed.

They tried out several rides, none of them especially thrilling, but Evans loved it. Primo spotted an ice cream stand and begged for a cone.

A plane hovering in the sky caught Mio's attention, but Primo was more interested in cars, so Mio and Evans took to the sky and Primo, and his mother went on the merry-go-round.

"This doesn't feel very safe," Evans said when they went on board the plane mounted on a crane. "Man, it flies right over the roller coaster!"

"I'm here," Mio said, with a smile. "I'll keep you safe."

The strange, dinky little plane ride finished and Mio descended the stairs happily. Evans followed, and Mio turned to him.

"You're good for my soul, Evans. I know I must let my sister love her husband . . . but I hate him."

"I know," Evans said. "Hopefully, he will change. You have to give him a chance for a new start . . . a new day."

"Ah, Evans," Mio said. "You are so . . . romantic. You are like that man on Las Ramblas . . . you know . . . the Man of La Mancha."

"You mean I'm tilting at windmills?"

Mio touched his nose, nodding. "Yes, exactly."

"I think in our own way we both do, Mio."

"I think . . . I think you make me *want* to."

Mio was quiet on the way back to L'eixample after dropping Belen and Primo back at the Cortez house. Mio's mother fed them all homemade chicken soup and rosemary and garlic bread before scuttling them out the door. Barcelona might have been the city of night, but the Cortez family went to bed early. Very early.

"You want to go to a club?" Mio asked Evans. The sky was dark, the stars felt achingly close. The night felt warm and cozy, like a blanket.

"No, I'd like to be alone with you. Is that okay?"

Mio nodded. "I like doing that with you. I don't usually spend time alone . . . I always have to be doing something. I like being with you."

Back at the apartment, Mio unpacked the suitcase, leaving a pile of things to be taken to the cleaners the following day.

"You want a banana cabana?" he asked.

Before Evans could even ask what it was, Mio whipped up the frothy frozen drinks for them. They sat on the sofa, draped over one another, looking at Mio's artwork on the walls.

"There's no alcohol in this?" Evans asked.

"No, baby. Crushed ice, coconut cream, bananas, a little milk . . ." Mio smiled. "It is a dirty-sounding drink, but even Primo loves it."

Evans laughed. "It is a dirty-sounding drink. I love drinking it with you."

Mio leaned over and kissed him. "I had a lady who does feng shui come in here, and she told me my paintings are very sad. The men are either dying, like Saint Eulalia, or waiting for their special man." Mio indicated the Alvarez painting. "She said I needed to have paintings of two men together . . . to draw my lover to me. Well, I never did do it, but somehow you found me, guapo."

"Well, I love your art collection, and I love Saint Eulalia. I've been wanting to know, is it the original?"

"You love Saint Eulalia?" Mio looked at him. "What is it about her that speaks to you?"

"Well, I first saw this painting in a book. I loved it. I felt . . . I still feel the image of the birds surrounding her in death, the people all far away, watching . . . nobody coming close . . . I felt like people always get it wrong, but animals know. Animals know the truth." He glanced at Mio. "Does that seem weird to you?"

Mio shook his head. "I think that is a beautiful observation. We have a lot of birds on this property here. I watch them sometimes. When one of them is sick or dying, the others sit with it. A vigil. They are, I think the messengers of truth."

Evans studied the painting. "The rope around her little wrist where they cut her down is heartbreaking. I suppose all the saints stood up to churches at the time . . . to pagan beliefs . . . small-minded kings and governments . . . stood strongly for the principles they believed in. I knew she was a young girl and I find that strength . . . that resolve so inspiring."

"Me, too," Mio said, leaning forward. "This painting is the original. I am proud of owning it. I have a couple of others I am looking at that I want to buy. I want your opinion."

"Okay," Evans said thinking back to the photocopy of the Alvarez piece he'd seen in Mio's filing cabinet.

"Evans, I am not asking you now but I want to know . . . if I ever did ask you, if things work out between us, could you ever think of living here in Barcelona?"

"Without having to consult a feng shui expert I can tell you yes. In a hot, Spanish minute."

Mio grinned. "Then you and I, I think, we need some sexy bedtime, baby."

CHAPTER NINE

Evans awoke around two in the morning. He and Mio had jumped into bed and had a fantastic time together, falling asleep. Now he was alone and for a moment, wondered if Mio had gone out and left him here.

He got out of bed and walked down the hall. He found Mio in his office, typing madly on his laptop, a single desk light illuminating his handsome features.

"Did I wake you?" Mio asked, looking up. Evans shook his head.

"Can't sleep?"

Evans yawned. "My baby left me alone."

Mio laughed. "I would never leave you alone for long. My hands would kill me." He swung in his chair. "Guapo, I have a client who is coming to Barcelona the day before you leave for Los Angeles."

Evans blinked. Last night, Mio was asking him if he would move here, now he was thinking about the day he would be leaving.

"And?"

"He's a rich guy. Married . . . bisexual. He has a boat . . . he likes to bring his friend as his . . . beard. We have lunch on the boat, he and I fool around, and then we come back to the harbor."

"And he wants a threesome?"

Mio shook his head. "No, but I would like to have you with me. You can talk to his friend when I go into the cabin to take care of business."

Evans thought about it. "Okay." He shrugged. "If you want me with you."

"I always want you with me." Mio's gaze was intense. "So I tell him yes?"

Evans nodded. "Any other bookings coming up?"

"They can wait until you leave."

Evans felt dispirited but hoped it didn't show. He really had fun in Portofino, but he didn't like the idea of this on a long-term basis. He didn't like it at all.

"Don't be sad. I love you," Mio said.

"I love you, too."

Mio wanted to take a run, but Evans wanted to check his emails and see if he couldn't contact Michael. It burned him that his assistant wasn't returning his calls.

"Come and sit here. Use my laptop. Use my desk." Mio pointed at his chair. "The chair is mine, that hot ass of yours is mine. They belong together."

Evans stood, kissing Mio, who pulled away as his cock began to harden.

"If we start this, I'll never go for a run."

He left Evans alone, and as Evans accessed his emails, he thought about Michael's silence. Something was up. Love had swallowed Evans up for a couple of days, but this wasn't like Michael.

"You need your phone?" Mio returned and handed Evans his cell. He was dressed in sweats and looked like a million bucks.

"God, you are the sexiest man ever," Evans said.

"Nice try, but I'm still taking my run." Mio blew him a kiss with his fingertips. Evans laughed. He loved Mio's sense of humor.

"Mio." His lover turned around again. "I can't get hold of Michael. He has a special ring on his phone for me. Even if I disguise my number, he will know it's me."

"Use my landline." Mio stood, waiting. "I want to hear what he has to say."

Before Evans could dial, the phone rang. He handed it to Mio.

Mio shook his head. "You can answer it, guapo."

Evans was surprised to find it was his housekeeper, Stella.

"I tried your cell phone," she said. "I didn't want to leave a message. This was one of your emergency numbers you left me." She took a deep breath.

"It's my housekeeper," Evans told Mio.

He frowned. "Is everything okay?"

"I couldn't call before," she said in a rush. Stella was Mexican by birth but spoke fluent English. When she became agitated, she spoke Spanish, and although Evans knew enough basic words of the language, he hardly understood a word she said when she went off on a tangent.

"Put her on loudspeaker." Mio moved forward and pressed the button. He asked Stella to repeat what she'd said. Evans understood the words *Nora North,* and his heart sank.

"What about Nora North?" he asked, and Mio held up his hand. He asked Stella a few more questions and finally looked at Evans, his eyes filled with pain.

"Michael took a job with Nora North. She has a new TV series starting, and he is now her assistant. He left your house. Stella said he and Nora had a party there and the house was a mess. She says Nora is using again."

Mio shook his head as Stella kept talking.

"Michael moved out. He and Nora came back very drunk yesterday, but he lost your house keys, and he couldn't get in. Stella wouldn't let him in."

"My God." Evans gripped the edge of the desk.

Mio said, "I think she should have all the locks changed

just to be safe. She should stay there. She says she can if her husband can join her."

"Of course he can. Evans spoke to Stella. "You still have the credit card I left you for emergencies?"

"Sí."

"Then please have all the locks changed."

"Sí, sí."

"I'm sorry this happened, Stella. Really I am."

In English, she almost shouted, "I'm sorry, Evans. Michael is a very bad man. And you are so good to him."

Mio gave her his cell phone number. "I want you to be able to reach us any time," he said. He gazed at Evans's stricken expression. "Are you okay?"

"I'm fine." *I feel like I just got shot in the stomach.*

"If he comes back, I will call the police," Stella said.

"You do that," Mio said and ended the call. He came over to Evans' side of the desk. "Run with me. It will do you good."

Barcelona on the cusp of dawn felt like a hidden archangel, all color, lights magic, and a hum in the air from the music playing in people's houses and in the clubs. Evans kept pace with Mio, and when they stopped at Las Ramblas and saw Don Quixote with his lance pointing to the sky, Evans wished he'd brought money to give to the man.

"We will come back later," Mio said and gave him a fierce, loving kiss. "I know you feel hurt, guapo, and I am sorry. I hate this man, and I hate your sister for doing this to you."

They ran back home and showered. By the time dawn broke, they were on their second pot of coffee, reading the morning papers together.

"My Spanish isn't good enough," he told Mio.

"Then I read to you." Mio pointed to an article on the

front page. "I translate. The archbishop wishes to have sex, so he is having sex with everybody. Sex, sex, sex."

Evans laughed. "What about the article next to it?"

"What do you know? This man wants to have sex, too."

"This man wants to have sex," Evans tapped his chest.

Mio laughed. "I'll give you sex, but first we go someplace wonderful for breakfast."

Evans touched Mio's face in wonderment. "I love you."

"Yeah, you should. I am a sweet guy."

Evans laughed again as Mio tried dressing him. "You're putting the wrong shoes on my feet."

"When we have babies, you will have to dress them," Mio said.

The idea tickled Evans more than he could say.

Mio took him to a local patisserie called Mauri, that even at six-thirty in the morning did a bustling trade. Housed in a medieval stone building, it was very elegant inside with its butter-colored walls and gleaming glass display cabinets of every type of pastry imaginable. Mio and Evans went for the chocolate croissants, which Mio assured Evans were the house specialty for over seventy years.

They sat outside, ate two pastries each and walked home hand in hand. Evans licked some chocolate from his lover's lips.

"We call this sloppy seconds where I come from," Evans said.

"We call this stealing food here in Barcelona," Mio said, making Evans laugh.

Back home, they fell into bed, and Mio began sucking Evans's cock. Turning around so he could suck Mio as well, Evans savored the softness of his lover's skin. He fondled Mio's ass and moved his mouth to it. Mio moaned. Evans licked and sucked, slipping two fingers inside Mio's ass. Mio's body tensed with desire. His cock hit Evans's chin,

Mio moving his fingers down to get it inside Evans's mouth. Mio moved two fingers inside Evans, and they came together, hard.

When at last they released each other's cocks, Mio said, "We always come together. Guapo, you are hot. Like fire."

They fell asleep, sprawled against one another. Evans awoke a couple of hours later with full sun on his face, Mio kissing his eyes and mouth.

"Evans, you ever been limin'?" Mio asked him.

He grinned. "No, what's limin'?"

"It's what the locals do in Anguilla. They lie around under the lime trees. I'd like to take you there."

"Anguilla? In the Caribbean? I've never been there. I've been to St. Martin which is near there."

"Ah, but Anguilla is a world away. I have a special bank account there. I would love to take you there. Nobody on the beach but us."

"Limin'."

Mio smiled, his face so breathtaking in the morning light. "Exactly. We go very soon. I promise."

They got dressed, ready to face the day. Mio handed him a check as they grabbed clothes for the cleaners.

"What's that?" Evans was stunned to see it was for ten thousand US dollars.

"Your fee for Portofino."

"Get out of here. I don't want your money." He was dismayed to see disappointment flash across Mio's features.

"It's your money, guapo. You earned it. This is business. Quite separate from our pleasure."

"I don't want it. I did it for fun." Evans was staggered at the high sum. He hadn't received anything like that for hours and hours, weeks and months of work on a screenplay as a writer, before he got in the Guild.

Mio still held it out. "I have an idea. Put it in the limin'

135

fund," Evans said, and Mio laughed.

"Now we have to go," he said.

They slipped into a beautiful routine of galleries, museums, shops, and beaches during the day, with lunches in between at Mio's mama's house. Evans took to calling her mama, too. He even looked forward to having his cheeks pinched. It made him feel loved. His afternoons with Mio were spent with Belen and the children. Mio showed Evans all the local bookstores, and he hunted for anything he could find that he thought would be impossible to buy in the States.

The bookstores were gearing up for La Díada de Sant Jordi.

"You'll see, baby. It's a wonderful tradition. All the bookstores bring out tables of their finest books and the flower sellers bring out their most . . . beautiful roses. The stores are open for twenty-four hours." Mio explained it was customary in Barcelona, mandatory in fact for a woman to give the man she loves a book on that special day. The man in return gave her the most perfect rose he could find.

"I think that is so wonderful," Evans said. "In America, they close bookstores every single day. Here, you have a love festival for them."

"Oh, it's been going on for hundreds of years," Mio said. "Hey, baby, look at this book." Its title, *How to Change Your Life Without Getting Out of Bed.*

"I could have written this," Mio said, looking disgusted. "Any hooker could."

This struck Evans as so funny, he couldn't stop laughing. It became contagious. Mio laughed, too. Others around them began to laugh, even though they didn't understand the joke. They stumbled out onto the street.

"You know what's not funny?" Mio finally said. "If I

hadn't gotten out of my bed in that hotel in London, I never would have met you."

Mio had a way of saying things that drove Evans's emotions to new and dizzying heights.

The couple's evenings were always their own and Mio took Evans to all his favorite places. They hit a few tapas bars and a couple of gay clubs, but Mio, like Evans, seemed to enjoy their long, romantic evenings together.

One afternoon, Mio napped on the sofa after a particularly big lunch, little Primo nestled in his arms. Evans didn't feel sleepy, so he told Mama he was going down to the family shop with Enzo who didn't feel like napping.

Aldo didn't seem any happier to see Evans than he had the last time, but grunted a reluctant, "*Hola.*"

The two brothers began to talk, and Evans strained to pick out words. Either he was getting to be a better linguist, or they *wanted* him to understand.

"I love cards," he said, desperate to bond with Mio's dad. "You want to play cards?"

"Sí, sí." Enzo clapped him on the shoulder. "You know *chinchon?*"

Evans's heart sank. "No, I don't."

"We teach," Enzo said, pointing from himself to his brother.

They hurried him into the secret back room and produced a pack of playing cards.

"You learn now," Enzo said, and after a few rounds, Evans realized the object was to get rid of your cards and have low points.

The men became infuriated when Evans reached a hundred and one points. A according to the crazy rules of *chinchon,* it meant the game was over.

Aldo shook a finger at him.

"Sorry," Evans said. "I didn't mean to."

He felt blessed relief when Mio appeared in the doorway.

"What are you doing, guapo?"

"Getting my ass kicked. I'm losing big time."

"You're playing *chinchon*?" Mio grinned. "Move over, Evans, the *chinchon* king, is here."

Evans sat back and watched Mio roll up his pants to his knees, the way his father and uncle did.

Aldo ran off and made coffee for them all. Mio shuffled the cards and dealt them out with the dexterity of a card shark. The game became a lot easier with his lover explaining the rules in English, but still, Evans lost. He did, however, develop a fondness for the game and the four men met again the following day.

It was on the third day that Mio once again slept on the sofa after consuming an entire apple and cherry pie with Primo, that Evans returned to the store. Aldo and Enzo were furtive and exchanged nervous glances. They took Evans into the back room with words, "No tell Mio."

He saw a tall, gangly guy with dark hair and glasses sitting at the table, waiting.

"I'm Gilberto, Belen's husband," he said in good, but heavily-accented English. "You must be Ay-van."

"Yes, I'm Evans. I'm very glad to meet you. You have a wonderful family."

Gilberto nodded, rocking back and forth, sucking on long, wet strand of his hair.

The four men played, and Aldo clapped Evans on the back.

"You get better." He smiled, and Evans stared. Mio hadn't been kidding. The guy had teeth like ancient ruins.

Gilberto seemed edgy after a few rounds. Evans was dismayed to see Enzo slip him some euros and Gilberto excused himself.

Aldo ignored the exchange, shuffling his cards. Gilberto

palmed a candy bar from a shelf. He gave Evans a friendly wave, but the whole thing hit Evans the wrong way. There was something about the guy's gait. Evans's gaydar was never wrong. He had the peculiar feeling that Belen's husband was gay.

He felt disloyal not mentioning the incident to Mio, but also felt in doing so, his fragile new relationship with Enzo might be destroyed. He had no choice. Mio knew something was wrong and wouldn't let up until Evans told him.

"You did the right thing, to tell me about it." He paused. "Now you know why I am mad at my sister. He is gay or thinks he is. Guapo . . . you can never tell her this, it would kill her, but he made a pass at me."

"What did you do?"

Mio looked affronted. "I rejected him. What else would I do? I am a whore, not a complete slut. Belen was pregnant with Primo and Gilberto came on to me very hard. She knew he was confused . . . she knew he liked men. He was—how do they say in porn?—a curious bisexual. I would say he is probably bi since he still likes to sleep with my sister, but she has never made him get tested for HIV, and he is a drug user. She has been tested, and she is fine so far, but if he brings any diseases home to her, I will kill him."

Evans was grateful Mio trusted him with the truth. He became determined to help Belen, remembering he still had some chapters of her work. Maybe if he could help her get published, her self-esteem would improve, and she wouldn't feel the need to stay with such a louse.

"She loves him," Mio said. "But he loves drugs . . . he loves his crazy life more. I believe she is his anchor, you know, but it is not enough."

It was on the tip of Evans's tongue to ask Mio if he thought Evans could ever be enough, if any one man could be enough for Mio, but their relationship was in a different place. They were not longtime lovers, with children and baggage. Evans wanted more than anything to be enough. *Time, I have to give Mio time.*

"Your sister is a dirty girl," Evans said, much later, sitting up in bed.

Mio, draped over him in his sleep, awoke, his eyes shifting into focus. "She is?"

"Oh, yes." Evans held up the pages he'd been reading. "She has written erotic romance . . . not only that, it's gay erotic romance. Mio, it's very, very good."

Mio laughed, scrubbing at his eyes with the back of his hands. "My sister writes good sex?"

"Baby, if I didn't know she was a woman, I would swear a man wrote this."

"Really?" Mio's expression was gleeful. "That's because I tell her these stories."

Evans lowered the pages. "You did?"

Mio shrugged. "She loves my stories."

"Are they real stories?"

Mio reached up and stroked back Evans's hair. "Yes. But I have never told her *our* stories. I love you too much, Evans."

"I can help her get published. Mio, she has to write a happy ending."

"But of course." Mio's eyes twinkled.

"There's always a happy ending," Evans insisted.

"You're so romantic, Evans." Mio drew Evans's head down to his. "Your boyfriend would like a happy ending right now, please."

Evans scooted down the bed to kiss Mio's hungry mouth.

They were interrupted by Mio's cell phone ringing by the bed. Mio grabbed it, checking the readout. "Sorry, guapo, this is about my present for you on La Díada de Sant Jordi . . . good roses are like good men. Very hard to find."

He ran from the room, and Evans began to worry. What kind of a book was he supposed to buy for Mio? Or was he supposed to buy him roses, too? And if so, what if his weren't good enough?

Suddenly the biggest romantic day of Barcelona's year loomed ahead like a frightening chasm. Who could he ask? He lay back against the pillows, touching the space where Mio had recently lain. It was still warm. He wished with all his heart he could bottle the feeling and the smell of Mio. Bottle it and keep it, to open whenever he needed it most.

CHAPTER TEN

The problem of what to get Mio for La Díada de Sant Jordi solved itself the next afternoon, two days before the big event. Almost two weeks had passed since Evans had arrived and he dreaded the day he would have to leave Barcelona. Mio hadn't suggested postponing his departure. In fact, they never discussed it. Evans had enjoyed thinking it was because the subject was too painful, but now over the family's lunch, Evans found himself brooding about what to do for Mio for the big day of romance. He wanted to give Mio something unforgettable . . . but something only he could give Mio. A tall order, he knew, but he pondered the problem as the others chatted about all the stores now being open.

Evans hadn't had a chance to talk to Belen, whom he had come to think of as his co-conspirator. He had put her in touch with a publisher friend who had requested the first fifty pages of Belen's book plus a complete synopsis via email. Evans had helped her with that. Even he had become misty-eyed at her lovely, happy ending. Now they awaited the publisher's response, and he was just as nervous as Belen. Over dessert, her cell phone rang, and she checked her text messages. She said nothing, but as soon as they were clearing the table, Enzo left the house with a cursory wave.

Belen elbowed Evans. "You must meet my father and uncle at the store. They want to speak to you."

Evans and Mio had planned a trip to the toy store with Primo.

"That can wait. You *must* go. I'll keep Mio busy."

Evans was nervous. What did they want? He hurried to the store and found the two brothers waiting for him. Gilberto walked toward them from the other end of the street.

"*Hola*," Gilberto said, extending his hand in greeting.

Evans shook it. "*Hola*, Gilberto." They all walked inside. Mio's dad had been doing well-selling roses and carnations as well as heart-shaped chocolates.

"They want to make sure you understand what a big day La Díada de Sant Jordi is," Gilberto said.

Evans nodded. "I understand."

The other three men exchanged glances. Gilberto spoke again.

"It is the custom for the woman to buy the man a book. Um . . . since you are both men, this will be your duty, since Mio is you know . . . the husband between you."

Evans might have been insulted had the situation not been so endearing and quaint.

"Okay," he said. *When was it decided Mio is the husband?*

"They want to know what book you plan to buy Mio."

Oh, God. "Well, I've been thinking about that and —"

"It must not be . . . um . . . ah . . ."

"Spit it out, Gilberto." Evans was curious now.

"It can't be a sexy gay book. No nude pictures. It must speak of your love for him."

Evans nodded, fascinated.

"It will be exchanged in front of the whole family over dinner. So it must be a good book."

Evans bit down a wild hoot of laughter. "Well, I have a book in mind, but I have no idea where to find it."

"What is it?" Gilberto asked.

"I would like to buy him a very old, very beautiful copy of *Don Quixote.*"

The three men looked pleased, but Enzo — was it Enzo?

Evans couldn't tell since his mouth was closed, his teeth hidden—said, "*¿En Ingles o Español?*"

"*Español*," Evans said. "I tried to read it once in English, and it was not good. I believe it is a lovely book in Spanish."

The men exchanged fast words.

"They will help you find a copy. It might be expensive."

"I don't care. I love Mio."

The words hung in the air. It felt like everybody held their breaths, but the moment passed. All the men hugged him, and he could have sworn Gilberto was trying to feel him up as Evans pulled away.

Enzo ran to the secret back room. "My father-in-law is going to find the book for you. They will call me, and I will call your cell phone with any news," Gilberto said. "I think you have chosen a very nice gift."

"Thank you," Evans said.

Gilberto's phone rang. "It's Belen. Mio's on his way down here. He and I . . ." He sighed. He slipped out of the store at a run.

Evans busied himself looking for paper to wrap his book. There were plenty of rolls available. He hadn't had a chance to select anything when Mio arrived. "So secretive," Mio said as his cell phone rang. His hand cupped Evans's butt as he said, "*Hola*, Stella. *Como es todo?*"

"Is that my Stella?" Evans asked him, shocked.

Mio nodded and squeezed his butt harder.

The call didn't last long. At Evans's inquisitive gaze, Mio shrugged. "I like her to check in with me and let me know everything's okay." He smiled at Evans. "I must take care of my one and only guapo."

Evans couldn't stop grinning. European men . . . they were a whole different breed.

They picked up Primo, who didn't like his new shoes and threw them out of the open-topped car several times as they drove into the city. Three times, Mio stopped the car, and each time, Evans found them. The fourth time he only found one shoe.

"We'll buy him more," Mio said, but Primo kicked his feet, happy to have shed the pesky shoes.

Mio drove over something as he rolled away again.

"Baby . . . I think I killed the shoe."

"Yeah!" Primo shouted, throwing his hands in the air.

They hit three different toy stores, Primo reluctantly wearing his shoes, even the dead one, but Evans loved Songololo, which specialized in wooden toys. Evans watched as Mio and Primo built a house out of wooden blocks.

"He loves anything interactive," Mio said. "I am trying to get him interested in things he can do alone."

Primo threw himself on the wooden house, destroying it.

Mio tickled him and Evans's cell phone rang. It was Gilberto.

"We found the book."

"Fantastic," Evans said as Mio scowled at him. Evans ignored him, reaching for tiny notebook he always carried in his pocket for emergencies. His matching tiny pen was missing, but the shop assistant lent him one and even told him how to find the store in question.

As Mio and Primo kept piling up the purchases, Evans joined them.

"Mio, I have to go. There's something I have to buy."

"Is it my present?" Mio looked ecstatic.

"Can't keep anything from you, can I?"

Mio shook his head.

"Do you mind?"

Mio grinned. "No, I don't mind you buying presents for me, guapo."

Primo scrabbled around the floor with his wooden blocks.

"Why don't you meet me back at my parents' house. I

made plans for us tonight. I hope you're okay with them."

"I'm sure I will be."

Evans started to leave.

Mio looked hurt. "Aren't you going to kiss me goodbye?"

Evans dropped a kiss on his lips.

"Ay-vun," Primo shrieked and reached up to hug him. "*Beso, beso,*" Primo kept saying kissing Evans's cheeks.

"Don't be long," Mio said.

Evans took a taxi to Cervantes y Canuda, a secondhand bookstore on Canuda. He stepped inside and felt right at home among the literary titles and found somebody who spoke English. She knew nothing about his special order, but quickly found somebody who did. He followed the man, who walked with a stoop into a back room and pointed to two volumes on a wooden table. He handed Evans some white cotton gloves and a magnifying glass. One book was in wonderful shape, the papers gilt-edged. The cover felt thick and heavy, but Evans felt drawn to the other, which had a bit more wear and tear.

The page edges were stained red.

"Egg wash," the bookseller told him.

The cover was green and had a soft, leathery texture. It wasn't immediately as striking as the first book, but it hooked him. It had color plates, which alone sold Evans, knowing Mio's love of art.

"This is from the nineteenth century," the bookseller said as Evans examined the exquisite print. "These are fine reproductions of the works of Honore Daumier."

"This is the one," Evans said.

The man nodded. "It is a charming book. It comes with a certificate of authenticity. It is from the private collection of one of our most esteemed priests whose family purchased in 1890."

Evans took a deep breath. "Where can I buy cotton gloves and a magnifying glass?"

The bookseller beamed. "I can sell you some right here."

He wrapped everything for Evans, then Evans sailed out of the store thinking he had never spent so much money on a single gift . . . nor enjoyed it more.

Hugging the store bag to him, he couldn't wait to give it to Mio. He walked for several blocks, wanting to be alone with his thoughts and his beautiful purchase. He walked longer than he realized, arriving at Las Ramblas. He sought out Don Quixote and put some euros into his wooden cup.

Don Quixote saluted him, and Evans smiled back, flagging down a taxi to take him home.

Belen greeted him at the door. "Want me to hide this in my room?"

"Please. Any word from the publisher?"

"She said she would read it today and get back to me by the weekend. Oh, Evans, I am so excited."

"Me, too." He hugged her. He tried not to feel upset that he wouldn't be here by the weekend.

She took the shopping bag into her room and Evans went to find Mio.

"Ready to go, guapo?"

The living room looked like a ransacked toy shop. Evans wanted to stay and play, but Mio clearly had other things in mind. As they drove home, Mio reached for his hand.

"We have to hurry. We have a plane to catch to Madrid."

"Madrid?"

"I forgot. I am doing a live sex show tonight with Biktor Bono. All I want is a romantic evening with you."

"Michael mentioned that show. I guess I'd hoped it was a horrible dream. Are you kidding me that we have to fly *now*?"

"No, guapo. Are you okay with this?"

"Biktor Bono is huge, Mio . . . like a big star . . . and he has a huge cock."

"I know."

"Will he fuck you?"

"If he can keep it up. Are you okay with this?"

"I . . . I guess. Wow . . . how could you forget this show?"

Mio poked his tongue out at him. "Guess I've been busy."

"You . . . you don't look happy, Mio."

"I'm not." Mio let out a breath. "I used to date him. A long, long time ago. Just so you know. But he is a drug freak . . . a real burn-out. I think he will be so out of it, this will be a nightmare. I agreed to do this to make him some money . . . before I even met you."

Evans saw the stricken look on Mio's face and forgot about his own qualms.

They raced home, and Mio rushed around getting ready. "We'll stay in Madrid at a motel tonight and come home tomorrow." Mio packed what looked like a flag and a minuscule pair of red briefs into a small overnight bag. He packed his oils, a disposable anal douche, toothbrush, and a pair of flip-flops.

"What will you need?" he asked.

Evans threw in a few toiletries, underwear, and a shirt.

Mio selected Evans's travel wardrobe. It was a see-through gold-colored shirt and one of his own pairs of brown leather pants.

"You look hot. I want you to wear these boots with them."

The boots were snug, but Evans was on fire now at the thought of the sex show. He'd never been to one, and his boyfriend was the star of it.

God, there's a little whore in me, too.

They drove to the airport and parked, arriving at the Air Europa departure gate for their flight with minutes to spare.

The flight took an hour and ten minutes, and the moment

they arrived, Evans knew they were no longer in Kansas. Madrid seemed to be wall-to-wall hot guys in love. With each other.

He and Mio took a taxi to the club, called Electra, where a drag queen waited out front. She kissed them both, cupping their crotches.

"Ooh, so sweet and juicy," she crooned.

"Hey, that's *mi marido*," Mio said, laughing.

She responded by kissing Evans on the mouth.

"Guapo, this very bad girl is Queen Estella."

"Pleased to meet you," she said, extending a velvety hand.

"I booked you into the Calypso Inn. Room number nine. It's away from the noise, and you will like it. All men." She handed them a key card. "You ready for dinner?"

"Sí." Mio took Evans's hand.

Things happened so fast, Evans thought his head would spin off its axis.

Hot guys kept arriving, kissing, groping one another, making jokes, each guy hotter than the last.

Dinner turned out to be at Queen Estella's mom's apartment overlooking Chueca, the gay quarter.

"My mother doesn't know I do porn," Queen Estella whispered as they climbed the stairs. "She thinks I am a singer."

Evans and Mio exchanged amused glances.

"Wait until you see the show," Mio said under his breath.

Evans was surprised to find Biktor Bono sitting on the balcony smoking a cigarette. He was as good-looking in real life as he was on camera, except he was also, quite clearly, stoned.

"Biktor, this is my husband, Everest," Mio said.

"I can't shake, I have a blunt in the other hand," Biktor said, and Evans was surprised to find he had an American accent.

"I fake the Russian thing," the big hulk said.

Biktor was sullen and silent through dinner, but Evans suspected the guy was so stoned, he didn't know what was going on. Everybody else mowed through salad, soup, pasta, and coffee and prepared to hightail it back to the club.

Evans noticed Biktor kissing Queen Estella's mother's cheek. It was an endearing gesture.

Biktor intrigued him, but he felt no jealousy, in spite of a previous relationship between him and Mio. Biktor was in his own, unhappy little world.

Fans were waiting outside the club for entry. Evans noticed a flyer on the ground with Biktor and Mio's photos promoting their big night. Mio took Evans's hand as they ran in through the back way. He introduced Evans to everyone and Evans had a hard time keeping track of them all.

There were old-timers, new faces, first-time performers, drag queens, trannies . . . and everybody laughed, kissed, groped, and played around. In the stinky upstairs bathroom backstage, Biktor Bono sat, naked except for white jockey shorts, shooting something into his penis. It hurt Evans just to watch.

"Is that Viagra?" Mio asked him, peering around the open door.

Biktor nodded, releasing his cock from the ties around it. He put the syringe between his teeth and slapped his flaccid tool.

"I always get performance problems. I get nervous in front of an audience."

Evans wondered if the man's huge blunt earlier had anything to do with it.

"We may have to fake it, Alejandro."

"No problem," Mio said.

There was no dressing room to speak of, just one big

room where people snorted coke off the backs of their hands and fitted themselves into form-fitting thongs or jockstraps. Mio stripped naked in a quiet corner, a couple of newcomers clearly agog, anxious for a taste of his beautiful cock.

"Can I suck you?" one of them asked.

Mio grinned, glancing at Evans.

"Sure," Evans said, and two of them fell to their knees sucking Mio right there and then.

"I can't come. I have to save it for the show," he warned them, but they didn't care. They just wanted a taste of the great Alejandro.

Evans rubbed oil on Mio's body, allowing the sycophants to help him. Slick fingers moved over Mio's cock, balls, and ass, and he kissed Evans as one of the young things took his cock into his mouth again.

Mio slipped his red thong in place, put his feet in his flip-flops, draped the Spanish flag around his shoulders, and said, "Time to go, baby."

Evans packed the things Mio had removed into the travel bag, and the entered the backstage area shrouded in darkness.

Biktor seemed glassy-eyed and out of it in his black thong studded with diamantes. Half of them were missing.

"I'm hard and ready to go, and he's soft," Mio griped.

On stage. Queen Estella pretended to whip a row of naked go-go dancers.

Mio's hand shot out to Biktor's cock. "Biktor, we have a show, baby."

Biktor snorted coke off the back of some drag queen's hand.

"I'll be fine. The Viagra will kick in."

"Want me to fluff him?" Evans asked.

Mio grinned. "Get him ready for me, guapo."

The crowd was wild, enthusiastic, and constantly shouted

suggestions to the performers along the lines of *Fuck, fuck, fuck!*

Evans got to his knees, parted the black covering over Biktor's cock, which was massive even in its slack state. He started to suck.

"I'll go out and start, send him out as soon as he is hard," Mio said. "Kiss me for luck, guapo."

Evans raised his face and kissed him, Biktor smacking his cock against their faces. Evans tilted Biktor's body to the side so he could watch Mio dancing for the crowd. He almost choked. Under the lights, in the full glare of adoring eyes, Mio was so hot. He draped the flag around his thighs, between his legs, his hips swaying to Marvin Gaye's "Got to Give it Up."

The crowd loved it. Evans tried to concentrate on the block of meat in his mouth. Biktor rotated his hips, and Evans felt he was getting somewhere as the crowd screamed and yelled, whistling and calling. Mio gave Evans a quizzical look. Biktor's cock was coming to life. Evans gave Mio a thumbs up. Mio nodded to Queen Estella, who announced Biktor to the crowd. Tucking himself back into his thong, he gave Evans a pat on the cheek and ran on stage.

Mio and Biktor got it on hot and sexy as soon as Biktor reached him. They rubbed up against each other, throwing each other's thongs over their shoulders, taking turns sucking cock.

Biktor's cock was hard, but he looked petrified now. Mio kissed and fondled him, and Biktor got to his knees, sucking Mio's cock. They rolled around on the stage as Queen Estella called them naughty queens. Biktor picked Mio up from the stage floor and tried to fuck him from behind. Evans watched from a monitor and knew Biktor was not inside Mio's ass. Mio faked it beautifully, Biktor stroking Mio to an explosive orgasm, his come spraying over the guys in the front row.

They took their bows, Biktor running off stage with Mio in his arms, his flag trailing from his fingertips.

A couple of the guys who had sucked Mio's cock leaped at the chance to suck Mio again. He seemed so horny and so worked up, Evans let the guys share his cock. Mio came again, his hand on Evans's shoulder. He squeezed him as soon as he finished shooting.

"Take me back to the motel and fuck me," he said in Evans's ear.

Evans helped Mio dress, and they ran to the motel. Mio knew where it was but said, "It looks pretty bad. You wanna stay here?"

"I want to fuck you," Evans said.

Mio kissed his hand. "I got all ready to be fucked by that guy, and now I can't wait to have you inside me."

They found the room, entered without a problem, but the room was awful.

"This isn't Positano," Mio said. "Never mind, baby, I am so horny, I could die."

They undressed quickly and fell on the bed. There was a strange smell in the room, but Evans didn't care. Mio had never begged to be fucked. This was his first chance, and he hoped, not his last. Mio's ass was still slick from Biktor's juices. The poor guy had never had a chance to get off, but his cockhead must have leaked. Mio threw open his legs.

"Stick it in, guapo, please, please don't make me wait."

Evans didn't. He licked his lover's ass briefly, his cock ready to burst. He almost crowed with pleasure entering Mio's steamy hole. Mio held his legs wider, moaning as Evans sank his cock inside him.

"Oh, fuck me, Evans, fuck me," he said over and over.

Evans started to itch. Something was on his feet and thighs, but he didn't care. He focused on the task at hand and came inside his lover's hot ass just as Mio said, "Something bit me."

They turned on lights and were shocked to find the bed crawling with bugs.

"Nice place you bring me to, Mio," Evans said.

"Glad you like it, baby." They jumped off the bed and laughed.

Chapter Eleven

La Díada de Sant Jordi fever gripped all of Barcelona. Mio's mom had been cooking for two days. Evans had put off buying wrapping paper for his gift, thinking there was plenty at the family store. The night before the holiday, he and Mio spent it at the family house together. It had been an amazing evening with Mio's dad showing old family home movies and everyone sipping champagne.

Mio was a clown with a proclivity for pulling faces every time a camera was on him, but he was handsome even with some of his teeth missing as a little boy.

"I must burn this movie," Mio said at one point when he saw his bad eighties' haircut and wide lapels for his school dance.

Early in the morning of the big day, Evans slipped out of bed. He and Mio slept in separate rooms for modesty's sake. It tickled him that Mio had come to him in the small hours of the morning and raced back to his own bed. Evans ran to the family store. There was no more gift paper. There was practically no more anything. He panicked, thinking his great gift would be ruined. All that was left was white tissue paper. He found some red and pink water-based paints and bought those, too.

He ran home and found Primo ready for action in his crib, calling out to him. Evans hoisted the toddler out and took him outside. They held the tissue down with stones, and Evans squeezed the paints onto dishes. He used a sponge brush to paint some on Primo's hand and his own. They pressed them onto the papers. Over and over again, they made their mark. Each time a page was filled, Evans moved it to the side.

Primo loved the game, and when Belen came to find them, she took the drying sheets into her room.

Later in the day, before lunch started, Evans wrapped the book, gloves, and magnifying glass.

Mio's dad closed the store and ran home. It was an experience Evans would never forget. He gave his wife a beautiful, long-stemmed, blood red rose. Then another. They kept materializing, and she cried when he said there was one for each year they had been married.

She gave him a book on antique motorcycles, which he loved.

"My father owns three motorcycles," Mio told Evans.

"I had no idea."

"Of course not. He's forbidden to take you anywhere on them. He's a maniac."

Mio grinned as he watched his mother trying to find vases for her flowers.

Gilberto turned up at the kitchen door, Belen's excitement and surprise evident. It was almost poetic that she didn't have anything for him, but he gave her a rose. He kissed her hand and hugged and kissed his children.

"Hi, Evans," he said.

Mio raised his eyebrows at Evans.

Belen gave Primo a picture book, and the little boy gripped it tightly in his hands. Nobody was allowed to touch it or look at it, except his father. For all his transgressions, Gilberto's children loved him. He hugged Primo. But the big gift of the day was Evans's gift to Mio. He ran his hands on the paper.

"It's so beautiful, Evans."

"Primo and I made it."

"Yeah!" Primo shouted, holding up his hands.

"I love it. I almost don't want to open it."

But Evans coaxed him. "Open the other two first."

Mio looked at him quizzically. He opened the packages containing the gloves and magnifying glass.

"Oh, Evans," he whispered. "What did you do?"

When he opened the book at last, his face registered a myriad of emotions. "It's the most beautiful thing I've ever seen."

He put on his gloves, studying the pages. Little Primo wanted to look and loved trying on the gloves, which swamped his hands.

"I love it," Mio said.

Each member of his family passed it around, using the gloves, and Mio's mother kissed Evans's cheeks.

"You got the best present," Gilberto said.

"It's not over yet," Mio said, kissing Evans's cheeks, Continental-style.

His father chided him, and Mio laughed.

"Kiss him!"

Mio kissed Evans full on the lips, and everyone applauded.

"You have to close your eyes," Mio said to Evans.

Evans closed them. When he opened them again, a dozen of the most beautiful roses he'd ever seen, lay on his placemat tied off with a big red ribbon.

He lifted them to his face. Each rose had a luxurious scent. "They're gorgeous. They smell so good."

"That's not all. Open this."

Evans opened the envelope Mio handed him. It was a note saying once a month he would receive a dozen of the finest roses of the season. *From Mio, with love.*

"That's amazing, thank you so much, Mio," he said and kissed him. A part of him gagged on the words though. He was going to *send* him, not give him roses. He was going to *send* them. *To America.*

Evans kept a smile on his lips though and tried hard not to think . . . not to worry about the future.

"You're awfully quiet," Mio said on the drive home.

"I had a wonderful evening," Evans said. "Your family is wonderful."

"Totally wonderful. They show you ugly movies of me."

Evans laughed then. "Mio, you have a fabulous sense of humor."

"So do you. Say, you know where we've never been?"

"Where?"

"To the beach. We have beautiful beaches here in Barcelona. You know . . . we should, on your next trip, go to Sitges. It's a beautiful gay resort . . . but for now, we have this."

Evans tried not to think about his next trip . . . leaving Mio.

"You know, I have never given a guy head in a car before," Evans said.

"I bet you've had tons."

"Once or twice. Guapo . . . don't you want to walk on the sand?"

Evans thought he would show his lover how little he cared about walking on the sand. As Mio parked right on the shoulder of the road, overlooking the ocean, Evans pushed him back in his seat.

"Oh, Evans." Mio stroked his back and neck as Evans sucked on him through his unbuttoned fly on his jeans.

Evans heard the waves lapping against the shore, matching his tongue strokes to the sound. His sucking sounds started to turn them both on, he could tell by the way Mio tried reaching for him, but Evans kept his lover glued to the seat, captive in his mouth. Mio's ass rose, thrusting up each time Evans pulled back with his lips and tongue. He sucked, harder and harder, careful not to let his teeth anywhere near the sacred shaft. He squeezed Mio's balls through the denim and Mio went crazy.

He flailed against Evans's mouth, coming hard and deep in Evans's throat. Evans refused to give up his prize as Mio shouted.

His cry of "¡Mi dios! My God!" roared over the Atlantic. Mio slumped in his seat. Evans say back satisfied. He hoped Mio wouldn't forget this blow job anytime soon.

The next day, his last full day in Barcelona, they had breakfast at Mauri and fed the pigeons in Saint Eulalia's square. The last thing Evans wanted to do was accompany Mio on his boat trip with his hot date. It felt horrible, but he'd agreed to do it.

He packed his clothes and his fingers lingered over his roses. He hated to leave them.

"We can pack some in your suitcase and hopefully they will be there when you get home," Mio said.

Home. Evans kept reacting to every word. *Christ, can I act any more like a whiny little girl?*

Either Mio didn't notice, or he chose not to notice Evans's mood. They drove off the seaport of Barcelona.

"We'll be here for a couple of hours. Tonight, we have dinner just the two of us, okay?" Mio said.

"You have a lot of appointments booked after I leave?"

Mio didn't respond for a moment. "Yes, I do. I put off a lot of appointments to be with you."

"Thank you," Evans said. "Mio, I've had a wonderful time."

They arrived at the pier Mio seemed to know so well. He was dressed in jeans with a collared, blue T-shirt hanging outside. He wore sneakers and once again looked amazing.

Evans followed him, feeling sick to his stomach. He knew now he could do this only occasionally. The strip show had been fun, the threesome had been wild, but this wasn't the life for him.

As they approached the boat, two older, gross-looking men waved to them. Evans was surprised to see they must have been in their sixties. God . . . he wanted to grab Mio's hand and make a run for it.

"Oh, you look so sexy," one of them said.

Evans never got his name. He helped Mio on board and disappeared with him down to the cabin. Evans heard their laughter, the exchange of kisses. His face burned at the memory of Mio sucking his cock, guiding him to an explosive orgasm in bed the night before, fucking him in the morning. He could still feel Mio's cock inside him. He heard the loud, masculine sounds of unmistakable sex and helped himself on board as the other man stood there watching him.

"I'm Leo," the man said, not moving a muscle to shake his hand or assist him.

"Hi, I'm Everest."

Leo laughed, and it wasn't a pleasant sound. The boat hadn't moved. They were tethered to the pier, and he heard Mio's laughter as the man in the cabin talked in rapid Spanish.

Fuck.

"Would you like a beer?" Leo asked. "I can make you a *clara*, if you like."

"I would like that, thank you." Evans knew it was a beer that had been mixed with tonic water. It packed less of a punch than straight Spanish beer. He could hear the two men fucking down below.

"Are you a whore, too?" Leo asked. Before Evans responded, he said, "Lemon?"

"I'm a friend of Alejandro's and lemon is great, thanks."

"A friend? I see. So after last time, he brings his bodyguard?"

Last time?

"I would love to fuck you and listen . . . my friend downstairs . . . he's not using drugs anymore so he won't hit Alejandro anyplace anyone can see. He's learned his lesson. Alejandro made him wait a long time. What about you? Are you willing to play? I have learned how to hit so I don't leave bruises."

Evans freaked out completely when he heard a series of slaps below deck. He felt his body trembling. He heard a punch. An *oof*.

"Is he hitting Mi . . . Alejandro?"

Leo shrugged. "It's what he pays for."

Evans was beyond upset. He heard the sound of Mio's voice, telling the other man he was being bad. Maybe *he* was doing the punching. He took the drink from Leo's puffy fingers and sat away from him.

"Drink," the other man said. "Don't listen to them. They go like this for hours."

Leo was the most aggravating guy he'd ever met. He was boring and droned on and on.

"You're not drinking," Leo suddenly said, interrupting his own flow.

"I am taking my time," Evans said, suddenly feeling frightened. The look on Leo's face was murderous.

"You need to drink quicker," he said.

God . . . he's drugged my drink.

He was pleased now that the boat was still moored and anchored, but he wished he could hear Mio talk. He wished he knew that Mio was okay.

Leo lunged at him, throwing him to the deck. The drink went flying, and Leo's mouth clamped over his, his hands tearing at Evans's jeans. Evans fought him like a tiger.

"What the fuck . . ."

Mio was up on deck naked, pulling Leo off Evans. Evans

161

gasped for breath, crawling away from his would-be assailant.

"You're raping a call boy?" Mio asked. The guy he'd been with came up on deck, flabbier and even more grotesque without clothes.

"Alejandro . . . he will pay, it's okay."

Evans tasted blood, it poured from his mouth.

Mio dropped beside him, cradling his head. "We're going!" he shouted. "You promised me. You promised me it would be okay this time."

"Alejandro . . . please don't leave."

Mio ran below deck to grab his clothes.

Evans struggled to his feet. If this had been America, these guys would have been packing, Mio threw his clothes on.

"Let's go!" he shouted at Evans.

"He should have finished the drink," Leo drawled. "He wouldn't have remembered a thing."

Mio dragged Evans away from the boat.

"Run," he said.

He didn't have to repeat himself. They reached the car and jumped in, Mio removing a gun from under the driver's seat. Neither man followed them.

"Shit!" Mio thumped the steering wheel with his gun.

"What the fuck was that?" Evans fumed.

"Did he hit you?"

"He bit my tongue and my mouth. He threw me to the deck. Why did you do this? Why did we come here?"

"This man gave me a huge retainer," Mio ground out. "I gave him one last chance."

"And you let him hit you?"

"Hell, no. I was the one hitting *him*."

"Do you know what I went through on that deck, wondering if you were okay?"

"I didn't think he'd do anything with you there."

Mio looked shocked. His hands shook badly, and Evans removed the gun from his hands.

Evans started to cry. "I can't handle this."

Mio tried to snatch the gun from him. "I'm going to finish this."

"Are you crazy? You're gonna shoot them?" Evans held onto the gun. "Just drive away. Just get us the hell out of here."

They both breathed heavily, Mio focusing on the road.

"Are you okay?" he asked a couple of times.

"Mio, are you going to keep doing this?"

"Not with them, no."

"But you aren't going to stop?"

"No, why should I?"

"Because these guys were crazy. What if they hunt you down?"

"They can't find me."

"We were in trouble out there," Evans screamed.

"This is who I am." Mio smacked the steering wheel when they stopped at a red light. "I thought you understood this."

"I didn't know about it until two weeks ago. You threw me right into it."

"Yes, you said you wanted it. I was honest with you . . . I opened myself up to you, but now . . . I share my life with you, and you leave me after all."

"Mio, I thought you were in trouble. You never told me he might hit you or that you would hit him. His friend told me he hit you before."

"He's a liar, and he's crazy. Evans . . . I'm so sorry." He reached across the seat and pulled Evans's face to him.

"I'm jealous, and I'm scared. I'm sorry. I can't help it." Evans took a deep breath. "I really can't handle it. I can't stand the thought of someone hurting you. How do I know you're not going to get gang-raped or beaten?"

"I told you to come with me."

"But I'm going home tomorrow. What then?"

A car honked them, and Mio moved forward.

"I guess we live our lives, guapo. I guess we say goodbye. I can't help it either. This is my life, and I am not ready to give it up."

"Do you think you could ever be?"

"I don't know."

"Maybe I should leave tonight."

"Maybe you should."

Evans let out a breath. Perhaps it was better this way.

They returned to Mio's apartment, both men subdued and emotional. So many words could have and should have been said, but neither would say them.

"I want to say goodbye to your family," Evans said as he finished his packing.

Mio hesitated before agreeing to drive him to the family home one more time. Belen and the children were out, Mama was sewing and Papa was at the store, waiting on a family who seemed to be spending a fortune.

He gave Evans a friendly wave goodbye.

It was a huge letdown, all of it. Mio drove him to the airport and Evans strained to see Don Quixote at Las Ramblas. He was there, all right.

"I want to leave him some money," he told Mio.

"You've given him enough money," Mio said and stepped on the gas.

At the airport, Evans got out of the car. "I love you, Mio. I love Alejandro, too, but Alejandro leads with his head. Please tell him not to forget about your heart. I love your heart."

Mio turned his face away. He did a savage turn, almost colliding with another car and left Evans standing there, driving off with a roar.

Evans spent a long day at the airport on standby. He got the last flight out of town and spent a miserable time getting from Spain to London. At Heathrow, he spent several hours at the departure gate until he could board the flight to Los Angeles. He was boarding when Belen texted him with the news that she had a publishing deal. He texted her back. He wondered what Mio was doing right now. And who he was doing it with. He sat back in his seat and realized with a sickening reality that it was probably over with Mio.

And he had forgotten to bring home some roses.

It was not until he reached LAX that he picked up the trades and saw the headlines. Nora North was in a new sitcom for the CW network. Her new showrunner was none other than Michael, his former assistant. Talk about getting stabbed in the back, the heart, and every place else in between. *I'm a pariah in the business. I can't get a job, but she's back in action. Unreal.*

He grabbed a Super Shuttle, not minding the cloying smell of patchouli oil on the woman sitting next to him. At least she wasn't trying to rape him.

What is he doing now? Has he had sex since I left?

Evans thought about Nora and Michael and wondered how life had come to this point. He'd lost everything. Like Don Quixote, he'd entered his period of insanity . . . but how could it be? His goals were clear, his intentions pure. He realized he'd probably never see Primo or Violeta or Las Ramblas again.

I'll never feel Mio's hands on me again. No more long kisses, no more early morning coffees. No more guapo. He swallowed his urge to cry. He had missed his deadline on his health insurance, not that he cared anymore. He'd lost the desire for the business. He remembered the smell of roses at Las Ramblas. Oh yes, Mio was right, he was tilting at windmills again.

CHAPTER TWELVE

Evans arrived at his house late in the evening. Stella and her husband Steve were watching TV.

"I wasn't expecting you until tomorrow," she told him.

"That's okay. I'm sorry. I should have called."

The couple was sleeping in the guest room. He told them they were welcome to stay; in fact, he wanted them to. He took a long shower, then a bath. He spent the next morning lingering in bed. Stella shook him awake, full of smiles, wondering how his trip had been. She waxed lyrical about Mio and how nice he was, and kind . . . he hadn't called her in a couple of days.

Evans knew she'd probably never have another cosy chat with Mio again. *Damn. Why is my whole body aching?*

"He is crazy about you," she said.

Evans closed his eyes. *How am I supposed to live without him?*

"I bring you coffee. You have a lot of calls to make." She opened his shutters. The light was too bright, but the day would only bring darkness. "Your phone rings nonstop."

She handed him his portable landline, and he jotted down notes. On the top of the list were his parents who were in Victoria, British Columbia.

"Home tomorrow," his father said. "If I never see another garden as long as I live, I'll die a happy man."

Evans smiled to himself. The message was a couple of days old. He loved his parents — his adoptive parents, not his birth parents — but ever since he had taken Nora North into his life, relations with his parents had been strained.

There were messages from people looking for work, hoping for work, and flat out begging for it.

He reached for his cell phone. No return text from Belen. She must have known by now that he and Mio had a bad fight. No return messages from his agent or any of his friends whom he'd called during his layovers. Hollywood was a wicked town.

At least Stella still loves me.

Evans called his parents and left a message and sent them a text as well.

His father called back within minutes.

"How about a round of golf?"

Evans hated golf but always played it with his dad because it made him happy.

"Or, we could meet for an early dinner. Your mother's going to some purse party tonight."

"I'd love that, Dad, I've missed you."

His father paused for a fraction too long. "We've missed you, too."

They agreed to meet at the Smoke House in Burbank at six.

I wonder who Mio is screwing now.

Evans had a busy afternoon watering his garden. It wasn't the scheduled day for watering. California was on heavy water restrictions with watering allowed Monday and Thursday only, but his garden was in bad shape. It was his therapy. Don Quixote had his dreams, Evans had his garden. He pulled and plucked at weeds. A ladybug fell on his fingers, and he remembered the one he and Primo rescued. He thought his heart would break.

His father was already waiting for him when he arrived on the dot of six. Evans could see his dad, Bloody Mary in hand, staring at a table of loud revelers. Evans prided himself on punctuality, but his parents always arrived early to places and could make Evans feel like a slouch for being right on time. He'd been coming to the Smoke House with his parents from the time he was a very small boy. In fact, he could even remember the very table they'd been sitting when his parents first broke the news that he was adopted.

Evans hadn't particularly liked coming here ever since then and actually felt, when his father radiated no pleasure at his arrival, that there might be an almighty zinger coming on.

"Hey, Dad."

His father, Matt McCoy, didn't stand. He indicated the seat opposite him as if Evans might be likely to select the floor. Matt McCoy and Gloria Evans had been popular radio and TV writers in the sixties and seventies. They wanted a baby and bought one—Evans—in one of the earliest Hollywood baby broker deals. His parents hadn't been forthcoming about the exact details of his adoption. They didn't mention that Gloria's former friend Dina North had been his birth mother.

Evans pulled out his club chair and sat, thinking that it was amazing how the people he loved always held something back. His parents, Mio . . .

His father sipped his drink. "What will you have to drink?"

"Just some iced tea, please," he told the waitress.

"Before you run off, I'd like to order," Evans's father said. He scrutinized the menu. "If you'd been on time, Evans, we could have beaten the clock and had half-price prime rib."

Evans felt his cheeks flame. He'd been on time. His father's need for deals was legendary. His need to humiliate Evans only recent.

"It's only a few minutes after six, Mr. McCoy," the waitress said. "I'd be glad to let you beat the clock."

"Thank you," the older McCoy said.

Evans studied his dad as he put the poor waitress through the rigmarole of repeating their entire litany of salad dressing and sauces, though by now, he knew the menu by heart. The Smoke House was the kind of movie industry hangout that was never quite fashionable but never went out of style, either. His dad looked good. His graying hair and twinkling blue eyes gave him a distinguished look.

Evans ordered shrimp scampi and a Caesar salad.

"How was your trip to . . . Spain, wasn't it?" his father asked when the waitress left.

"Yes, it was. I had a great time. Did you know that they have a festival in Barcelona this time every month that —"

His father cut right into his words. "I think you should know, you've devastated your mother. All this Nora North nonsense. I mean . . . my God. That came back and bit you in the butt, didn't it?"

Evans braced himself. His dad rarely got mad, but he was mad now.

"All your life, you've been a dreamer, Evans. It used to get you into trouble in school. It's time you woke up and smelled reality, pal."

The waitress returned with a fresh drink for his father, Evans's iced tea, and their salads.

"Thank you," Evans said.

She gave him a sympathetic smile. *Oh, boy. The waitress feels sorry for me.* He looked around the room. Probably a lot of people could hear his father's raised voice, in spite of the loud party next to them.

Matt McCoy was on his semi-annual tirade about how hard he worked and how he'd scrimped and saved to support his family. This actually wasn't true, but Evans never said so. Gloria had inherited her parents' vast estate, and they lived in luxury, but Matt McCoy never appreciated the life his wife provided them all. In fact, he seemed to resent it.

" . . . so you can imagine, we had our dreams, too, Evans. You're not the only one."

The waitress rushed over with their entrees.

"Where's the fire?" Matt asked her. "You trying to get us out of here?"

"No, sir, but you always like your dinner hot, sir."

This was true. He even had the waitress acting nervous. She glanced over her shoulder at Evans, who signaled her for the check as his dad took a call on his cell phone.

His dad had always wanted to be a successful novelist and screenwriter. He looked down upon his own TV writing career, but never looked down on Evans. With his son, he'd always been encouraging and supportive.

Matt McCoy ended his call and glanced at Evans. "She wanted a baby badly, you know."

"I know, Dad." Evans toyed with his shrimp. It was nothing like the food in Italy. He missed Mio terribly. He missed his hands, his smile, sharing his bed. He wondered if Belen was writing and hoped she was. She had a lot of talent.

" . . . so you see, Evans, her dream was to have a baby, but she couldn't. So we adopted you."

Maybe his father hadn't meant it the way it came out, but it was harsh and cruel. His next words indicated he had meant it, and Evans handed the waitress his credit card as soon as she came back.

"So . . . like everyone else, you're gonna have to wake up and stop dreaming, Evans. Get back to reality, kid." He rattled the ice in his glass. "Damn, these drinks are too good."

Evans thought about Don Quixote whose passionate flight of fantasy, whose dreams vanished with reality. Don Quixote died, as the story went, sane, but severely depressed.

Dear Mio,

I don't expect a response, I just wanted to say a few things. I had dinner with my dad tonight, and he said that I am a dreamer. He said this as if it is a bad thing. I don't think it is, because if it were true that dreams are wrong, then I could never write. Painters could never paint . . . well, you get my meaning, I am sure. You once told me you think love is like music and you know what, so do I.

I regret nothing about knowing you, only the way we said goodbye. I have felt more alive and real in the dreamtime I have known you. I could never regret that. I miss you and I know I always will. When you see Don Quixote on Las Ramblas, please give him some euros from me. Keep your heart open and your body safe.

Do you know the song Dulcinea *from* The Man of La Mancha? *Don Quixote tells her she is like a prayer, that an angel has whispered to her . . . he has thought about her too long. He has dreamed of her and sought her, sung her and loved her. I want to thank you for waking up that part of me I'd allowed to fall asleep. I wish you a life of beautiful things. I hope one day to see your gorgeous face again.*

Evans

He hit the send button on his fax machine at three twenty-five in the morning. It had not been lost on him that Mio had always chosen to send him letters because Evans was a writer who loved words. He regretted the passion and pain in his letter, the honesty, the hurt. But he didn't regret loving Mio. He put the fax in his drawer and sat in his chair for a long time, trying to decide what to do with the rest of his life.

Evans found it easy to sleep once he went to bed at five, in spite of the excruciating evening with his dad. His house phone rang at seven, and he was surprised to find it was Mitch Radford, the studio executive he'd met with at Heliconia Films.

"Hey," Mitch said, "I know this is probably early, but I

just had a screenwriter bail out on me. I have a romantic comedy that's three-quarters done. It's a TV movie, but I think it might be right up your alley. Want to come in and discuss it?"

Am I dreaming? "Sure, I'd love to come in. When would you like to see me?"

"How about nine o'clock? Is that too early?"

"No, not at all. That's great, Mitch, thanks."

He breathed a sigh of relief. He wasn't so washed up after all. He called Kelly King, his agent, who cut him off before he could even tell her the good news.

"I can't represent you anymore," she said. "We just made a huge deal with Nora and Michael and part of the deal is that we can't represent you anymore."

Evans almost laughed. "Okay," he said. "Can I have that in writing?"

"I already sent you a letter. Signature confirmation. Sorry it worked out this way, Evans."

"Yeah, me, too." Evans wondered once again how it was possible that he was struggling to find work and yet Nora North, who'd wrecked an entire TV show already had a new one. Evans hadn't even begun to deal with the legalities of his show being stopped. He wondered if his attorney was still talking to him. He couldn't even step into Mitch's office without some sort of representation. Evans got up, showered, and made coffee then sent Alan an email asking him if he would handle the contract for the movie.

Of course, Alan wrote back. *Congrats, dude.*

At the studio, Mitch Radford took Evans into his office the second he arrived.

"It's a movie set in the Caribbean, and everything's gone wrong . . . but I figure anyone who can weather a crazy chick like Nora North can handle a few tropical storms," Mitch told him. "Here's the screenplay, what I have of it. Hard copy and CD. The treatment's on there, too, and ah . . . I need it in a week. I can give you notes and then we'll have you do a rewrite. Sound cool?"

"Very cool." Evans looked at the title page, *The Sand Dollar*.

"It's set on the island of Anguilla. Depending on the tax breaks they offer us we may or may not shoot some of it there, but the story is set there. I have photos for you, and I have the original book."

Mitch kept piling things on top of the screenplay. Evans left the office, and Alan called him a few minutes later.

"I got you a good deal. You're getting scale for finishing this, but you get a bonus on points and a look-see on your next project. So make this one good, dude. I'm going to petition the Guild to scrape you under the wire for health insurance. I'm so damned mad about what's happening to you, by the time I'm done with the Guild, your flipping agent, and the network, they'll all be lucky to get jobs at Starbucks. And oh, hey, you want to visit Anguilla when they shoot?"

"No," Evans said. Anguilla. He had planned to visit the island with Mio. The last thing he wanted was to run into him.

He should have been happy, and he *was* happy. How weird he was writing a screenplay set in Anguilla. He took everything home, sat out on the back sun deck and read. The original book by a woman called Sarah Anderson, was lively and captivating. The words were evocative, the author's autobiography of her decision to move to Anguilla and start a business was absorbing and funny.

When she lost everything in a hurricane, she rebuilt and sold her store for a profit, finding the man of her dreams. Perfect TV movie fodder.

The screenplay was not. Evans knew to make this thing

fly, he had to repack his snowball from scratch, as his screenplay guru William Goldman put it. For four days, he worked relentlessly on the screenplay. Somehow as he made notes, the dream man's face became Mio's.

He worked with minimal breaks until on the fifth day, it was finished. He called Mitch Radford, who was overjoyed. "Meet me for lunch at Craig's, let's say twelve-thirty," he said. *God, how industry-cliché could you get?*

Evans agreed to meet him. He printed a copy of the screenplay and also emailed it to Mitch. He showered and changed, his body aching from the grueling pressure he'd put himself under. He'd never once stopped thinking about Mio, but also never let it stop him. He knew one day the way he felt now wouldn't be the way he felt anymore. He picked out a nice suit and tie, thinking that if he looked elegant, it would make him feel a lot better. His shoulders ached, but he felt an accomplishment in his hard work.

It's a good screenplay, I know it is.

As he got into his car, his cell phone rang. Michael. His heart stopped. He was nervous about Michael showing up at his door if he was out. Oh, well, too bad, it couldn't be helped. He let it go to voice mail. Michael could wait.

Mitch was a fun lunch companion. He knew his way around Craig's menu and he and Evans both settled on ahi tuna tartare, splitting a mushroom truffle.

"Your parents were awesome writers. Do they do any work now?" Mitch asked.

Discussing his parents' work was easy for Evans. In their time they'd been brilliant writers, but even writers get old in Hollywood. The urge to make it by the time you were twelve was still there, even if you worked behind the cameras.

Mitch asked Evans out on a date. Evans said once their work was completed, he might, but he couldn't date his boss.

"So you're not seeing that Spanish porn star anymore?"

Evans gaped at him. "How do you know about . . . him?"

Mitch shrugged. "Your former assistant Michael. He's told everyone. Of course, I'm an Alejandro fan, and I'm having penis envy right now. He looks like he loves to fuck. Am I right?"

Evans felt winded. That was a sucker punch he hadn't been expecting. He couldn't talk about Mio this way.

"Sorry," Mitch said. "I think I just scratched an open wound."

Evans picked up his water glass. "Something like that."

"Fair enough." Mitch snatched up the check.

Evans drove home hoping that Mitch wouldn't sabotage his work on the screenplay because Evans had semi-turned him down. Michael had told everyone about Mio? Oh well, he didn't care who knew. Mitch knew and still gave him work. The funny thing about the gay community was that they loved their porn stars, idolized them actually, in a way that straight people did not love straight porn performers.

He listened to the three o'clock news. An accident on the freeway. Well, he was taking surface streets so it didn't matter. Then he heard the name. Nora North. She'd been driving the wrong way on the freeway, stoned, drunk, and apparently in a stolen vehicle, and hit four cars. Nobody was hurt, but apparently, her brand new nose was shot to shit.

Wow. Evans bit his lip. Now he knew why Michael had been calling. He obviously wanted his job back. Evans felt lighter than he had in days. He was aware of a vehicle behind him on Coldwater Canyon, following awfully close. He peered in the rearview mirror as the guy started honking him. A taxi. The guy kept pointing to the side of the road. No way, he wasn't pulling over so some freak could rob him.

"Guapo!" a voice shouted.

Evans almost drove off the road.

He pulled over, the taxi right behind him. Evans concentrated on breathing, his fingers gripping the steering wheel. He didn't think it could be true, but it was him . . . his gait lacked its usual swagger, his face was pale, but he was still beautiful. And anguished. Mio rapped at the passenger window. Evans lowered it.

"You don't answer my calls . . . you're dressed like that . . . have you met someone else?" Mio asked.

Evans felt the tears blinding him and shouted, "You stupid man. Who the hell could I love after loving you?"

Mio tried to unlock the door, but couldn't. Tears fell down his face, but he wriggled in through the window, and his mouth met Evans' in a kiss that Evans would never forget.

"I can't believe you're here."

"Believe it," Mio said. "I may be a whore, but I'm not stupid."

Evans laughed and pulled Mio all the way in. "What are you doing here?"

"What does it look like? I came on my horse, to take you home." Mio pulled Evans's head down to his and kissed him again. "I'm not very comfortable here, and I think if we take our clothes off we might get arrested."

"LAPD has some cute cops though, Mio."

"No way. I'm not interested in that crap anymore. I want you to come home with me, Evans. I want you to write. I want you to love me. I want you to help me figure out what I am going to do with the rest of my life, now I'm no longer going to be a whore. Don Quixote might have died sane but miserable. We're not going to do that."

"We're not?"

"No. You're going to show me this house of yours. Stella tells me you work night and day."

"Stella, huh?"

"Yeah. Guapo, I think you're getting hard."

"I think you're right."

"My sister won't speak to me, Primo is mad, my dad is mad, even Gilberto says he won't clean up until you come home, and as for Don Quixote . . ."

Evans smiled. "What about him?"

"He refuses to accept my money!"

Mio shifted around in the front seat, giving Evans kisses. Lots of long, lingering kisses. He unzipped Evans' fly. "You ever had a blow job in your car, guapo?"

Evans couldn't think.

"Your cock likes me," Mio said, coming off it for a moment,

Evans nodded.

"Your cock knows I love it back." Mio stroked the head with his tongue. "Guapo, do I have to beg for us to go home?"

"I think I've forgotten the way."

"No, you haven't." Mio raised himself on his knees in the passenger seat, taking Evans's face in his hands. "Home is right here. Right here with me."

"Not on your life," Evans said. "I'm taking you home."

"I'm not going to argue," Mio said, kissing him again.

"That makes a change."

The taxi driver honked.

"Oh. I almost forgot." Mio threw the passenger door open and ran back to the taxi. Evans gripped the steering wheel, watching him. *I can't believe he's here.*

He. Is Here.

Mio returned with a suitcase and a bunch of roses. He handed the flowers to Evans through the open door. "Don Quixote comes with a lance . . . I come with a reminder of the roses I love to give you."

He tossed his suitcase into the backseat. "I saw this man standing on a street corner selling these."

Evans put his face into the blooms. They had a faint smell, but it was enough. They smelled like love.

"He had bags and bags of oranges." Mio looked amazed. "But only these roses. They're not as nice as the ones in Barcelona—"

"They're beautiful, Mio. Thank you." He smiled, fighting for composure. "Trust you to find the only street seller in Los Angeles with the most perfect flowers in the world."

Mio nodded. "Sí, señor. Are we going home now?"

Evans joined the flow of traffic, Mio kissing his eyes, his nose, his mouth . . . making it difficult to see.

They made it home and fought over who was carrying the suitcase indoors.

"If you were a woman, I'd be carrying you over the threshold," Evans insisted. "Let me carry the suitcase."

"Why can't you carry me?" Mio asked, but his eyes twinkled.

Stella came running out of the house. "Señor Mio!" She threw herself into his arms.

Mio laughed and kissed her cheek.

"How do you know it's Mio?" Evans asked her.

"I've seen all his movies."

"You have? Man, I haven't seen a single one."

Mio touched his face. "Good. Keep it that way."

They went inside, and Mio moved straight to the TV, trying to fire up the remote.

"You want to watch TV?" Evans asked, stunned.

"No, guapo. I want to see your sister drive backward on the freeway again."

"It's on TV?"

Mio stared at him quizzically. "You haven't seen it? I saw it on my cell phone. It's all over the news. Look, baby, there

178

she is."

He laughed as the footage, apparently the rage on TV and the Internet, played on a seemingly endless loop. Nora, looking totally whacked-out, gripped the steering wheel, cigarette in her mouth, taking out cars left and right before coming to a skidding halt against the median wall of the 405 Freeway.

"Oh, my God." Evans fell onto the sofa beside Mio, who put his arm around him.

"You've been busy writing? Is that why you didn't see this?"

"Yes." Evans huddled closer to Mio who now seemed tense. Before he could ask why, Mio said, "And Michael? The assistant? You heard from him since she got arrested?"

"I have. He wants his job back."

"And?"

"I didn't even return his calls."

"You didn't return my calls either."

"I didn't know you called, Mio. I couldn't stand the thought of checking and not finding a message."

"You have a beautiful house . . . a whole life without me."

"So do you," Evans pointed out.

"Where do you write?"

Evans smiled. "Out the back."

"Show me."

He took Mio to his writing room. "This is where it all happens, eh?" Mio asked. "All the dreams . . . all the hard work." He touched the fax machine. "Our lifeline."

"Yes." Evans's voice was quiet. "Yes, it is."

"Guapo . . . what are you doing with this book?"

"I just adapted it for a screenplay?"

"You did? For a movie?"

Evans nodded.

"I know this woman, Sarah. She's a friend of mine."

"She is? Really? I wish I'd known that when I was writing the screenplay. How do you know her?"

"Her husband is a businessman in Barcelona."

"Oh, my God. Did you . . . you know . . . sleep with her?"

Mio looked pained. "I don't sleep with everyone, baby. Maybe half of Barcelona but not all of it."

Evans laughed.

"I know her from Anguilla. I introduced them."

Evans stared at him, tickled that Mio had played match-maker.

"You wrote this without doing any limin'?"

"No limin' for me, Mio. Not without you."

A shout from outside made Mio drop the book on the desk. They ran to Stella, who stood outside as Michael attempted to come up the side entrance to the office suite.

"Señor Mio. It's *him*!"

Mio's eyes narrowed. "The things you see when you don't have a gun."

Michael seemed to pale, and Evans rolled his eyes. "You and your guns, Mio. I'll talk to him."

Mio held him back. "No time for talking. I want to kick this guy's ass." He hunted around the garden.

Michael held up his hands. "I just want to apologize."

"Turn the hose on him!" Mio shouted at the neighbor next door, who was watering his garden, watching the confrontation.

The neighbor looked shocked. "You want me to squirt him?"

"Yes! He hurt my boyfriend."

"With pleasure." The neighbor hit Michael full bore.

Michael screamed and ran down the path, the blast of water following him.

The neighbor smiled. "I've been wanting to do that for months."

Mio leaned over the low fence, kissing the neighbor's cheek.

"*Gracias.*"

The neighbor smiled and turned to examine his angel trumpet trees.

Stella went back into the house, laughing.

Mio slipped his arm around Mio. "He won't be back, and I think Stella and her husband like having the house to themselves. I've been thinking. I have a friend who has a wonderful house in Anguilla. I think we should go there, spend some time, a few days. Making love . . . limin'. You think you would like to do this, Evans?"

"You know, I think I would like it. A lot."

CHAPTER THIRTEEN

"How do you like limin', baby?"

Evans arched back to Mio, laying warm and brown beside him on the chaise, naked under the sun.

"I love it, Mio. My research says that limin' involves lying underneath an actual lime tree doing nothing, but this is just as good."

Mio smiled. "Oh, you're so technical, guapo."

Evans laughed and sat up to look at the mesmerizing view of the boats bobbing out in the harbor. He could see Prickly Pear Cays and Dog Island in the distance. They kept making plans to take the boat moored to their private dock out there, but so far, it was hard enough to rustle up the enthusiasm to do anything that involved clothing.

The estate they were staying at was beautiful. Mick Jagger was a neighbor, but they had total privacy. The tropical garden, lavish with its cabanas and an infinity pool had plenty of space for nude sunbathing.

Mio stroked his back. "If it pleases you, we'll put a lime tree out here, okay? You just tell me where you want it."

Evans laughed. "Your friend who owns this might object to our rearranging things."

Mio's hand stopped moving as Evans reached for his cock, which hardened and glistened in the sun. Evans could never resist Mio's cock. He bent to suck it into his needy mouth. He loved pushing back the uncut foreskin with his tongue, savoring the prize of Mio's meaty cockhead.

"Actually," Mio said, moving his hips now. "I'm the

owner."

Evans stopped sucking and lifted his face.

"You are?"

Mio nodded. "I've been thinking. You want to write. I need a new ... focus. We should make movies and TV shows at home in Spain. I told you before, you are valuable in a place like Barcelona with all your experience."

"The language might be a problem."

"Why? You're learning Spanish, and you've got me. How does that song go? 'I've got the looks, you've got the brains, let's make lots of money.'"

"Hey, I've got some looks, too, you know."

Mio's hand moved to Evans' cock.

"I know you do. I love you. Look at me. I'm all squashed up here with you. My tan is uneven because I have to be close to you. I can't keep my hands and mouth off you. Think about it. We will call our company Guapo Films."

"That has a ring to it."

"Of course it does. And all we make are guapo films and TV shows."

"I'd need a work permit."

"We can fix that. And you can always marry me. My mother wants a big fat gay wedding, you know. Gay marriage is legal in Spain."

Evans laughed. "I love your mother."

"She loves you."

Evans felt incredible pleasure at the thought of making a step like this, with Mio.

"Of course ... we should discuss this idea over dinner at Cap Juluca."

Cap Juluca. It was the most exquisite hotel on Anguilla. They'd eaten there one night with Sarah, whose book Evans had adapted. She and her husband were staying in a villa with a Moroccan style dome, the bathroom so huge it had its own garden.

The restaurant jutted out over the ocean where the two couples made an evening ritual of feeding bread to jumping silver fish in the shallows.

"You think we should discuss it with Sarah?"

"She has some ideas about working on some things with you."

"Really?" Evans couldn't believe this enticing opportunity was his for the taking. Mio moved Evans's hand out of the way and got down on his knees between Evans's hot legs.

"Yes, really. And you could work with Belen on a nice, romantic movie."

Evans smiled as Mio licked a path across his groin. "It's hard to say no when you're licking me, Mio."

"Of course it is. Why do you think I keep my mouth so busy?"

Evans laughed into the blue sky.

"Say yes." Mio licked and sucked his cock, sounding testy all of a sudden. He pulled Evans' hands into his, putting Evans down onto the grass on his back. Evans' legs respond naturally, opening to Mio when his face dropped right between Evans's ass cheeks.

Evans put his feet on Mio's shoulders. Mio licked him faster, with genuine ferocity. Evans could feel his lover's hard cock jutting against his thigh, anxious for entry. Mio thrust into him quickly, his mouth moving up Evans's torso. Evans reached for Mio's face as his lover fucked him.

"Oh yes, Mio. Yes."

"Say it again."

"Yes, yes, yes."

Sunday in the Park with George
A. J. Llewellyn

Excerpt

When he finally stopped laughing, Kevin held out his hand to Lucas. That surprised him. They shook hands, Kevin grinning at him.

"Congratulations. Just as I suspected. You're a real weir-do."

Lucas winced. "I guess."

"You guess? Aren't you a chess champion? I'd expect you to read books on geometry or science maybe. But this . . ."

"I read those, too," he mumbled.

Coco wriggled out of Kevin's grasp, and he deposited her gently onto the ground. She sniffed around.

"Let me explain." Lucas took a breath. If I can.

Kevin held up a hand. "Oh, no. You can't explain that book."

"Yes, I can." He hurried through his explanation about how he and his father shared crazy book titles with one another.

Kevin listened. Coco pawed at his ankles, and he lifted

her onto his lap again.

I'm jealous. Of a little dog! I'm a sick man. Sick!

Lucas gave up. "Well, it's been . . . interesting but I really have to go now." He took hold of the dog again, and she rewarded him with tiny kisses. He excused himself, went back into the building and left Coco inside his parents' door.

He turned to find Kevin right on his tail. It unnerved him, to say the least.

"Where are they?" Kevin asked in a dramatic whisper.

"Probably shagging. They're newlyweds."

"Oh, cool. Let's drink all their booze."

Coco fought to get outside the apartment door. Lucas gently pushed her back inside, closing the door and locking it. Coco gave him a couple of indignant yips from the other side and then went quiet. She'd probably run straight into his parents' bedroom.

Kevin stood, looking uncertain. "You really have a date?"

Lucas sighed. "Yes, I really have a date."

"You're just saying that."

"No, I'm not."

He walked out of the building, Kevin beside him. The bar was only six blocks away, but he didn't want Kevin following him there. He flagged down a taxi, ignoring Kevin, who urged him to stay and talk.

"Have a nice night," Lucas said, locking the back door before Kevin could open it and jump in beside him. He had the absurd feeling he'd really upset the guy and that he was somehow being disloyal to him.

Oh, boy. I'm a wreck.

He arrived at Plus, a gay bar on the edge of his neighborhood, bordering the old garment district. Plus, which sat beside a shuttered art framing business, had a hard-to-find entrance around the side of the building, involving rickety stairs against a chainlink fence. Inside, he was pleased by his date's choice. The bar was decorated to look like an old-fashioned wine cellar. Candles lit the small space, and classical music tinkled from some hidden corner of the room. The menu was written on a chalkboard above the bar.

His date, David, who taught English as a second language to adult students, was older than his online photo and a lot pudgier than the 'few extra pounds' he owned up to in their brief phone call.

"I took the liberty of ordering you a glass of wine," David said. There was something off in his manner, and Lucas felt nervous. Why would the guy order him a drink before he'd even arrived?

He's spiked it. Damn it. This dating business sucks!

"It's an old world red, a Côté Catalanes," David said. "Go ahead, try it."

Lucas couldn't let go of the absurd idea that the guy had slipped something into his drink. He caught the bartender's eye.

"Is this as good as . . ." He hesitated, scanning the board, "the Medoc?"

"No," the bartender said, taking the glass away from the coaster in front of him. "Let me get you the Medoc."

David looked pissed. "That's a good glass of wine," he croaked.

"I like Medoc." Lucas had never tried it in his life. He almost croaked himself, forking over sixteen dollars for a wine glass only filled a third of the way. He hated this new trend. Consumers were getting ripped off all over the place.

"So tell me what you do." David had adopted a sulky tone to his voice.

"I can tell you one thing. I don't fuck on the first date," Lucas said, leaning in close. That was when he noticed David's dark hair was a wig. Wisps of white-blond hair poked from underneath the ill-fitting piece. Who the hell was this guy?

Lucas finished his drink quickly. David had already lost interest in him. He was scanning the room looking for fresh meat when Lucas bid him a goodnight and ran all the way home. He turned a couple of times to make sure the guy hadn't followed him.

He could hear wild laughter coming from inside his father's apartment as he unlocked the door. He was surprised Coco didn't come to greet him and felt an absurd stab of envy when he walked in and saw Coco in Kevin Morgan's arms. They were sitting at the table with Aleksandra and his father.

"They just invited me to hear the sonata," Kevin said.

"Great. When are we going?"

"Well . . ." Aleksandra blushed. "We only get to invite one guest, and we thought you were out for the evening."

"You mean you're taking him and not me?"

"We thought you were out," she repeated.

"Fine," he said, furious that Kevin had taken away the dog's affection and his invitation to the sonata. It was just like goddamned Salvatore all over again. That had been the hard part, breaking up with the guy when his parents had forged their own relationship with his lover. It was happening all over again only this time he didn't have a relationship with Kevin. He didn't have anything.

"Have fun," he said.

"Don't be silly," his father said. "We'll call Dominika and explain."

"We can't." Aleksandra looked scandalized. "She'll freak."

His father ignored her. Kevin sat back in his chair, clearly enjoying the sudden tension between his hosts.

Martin called Dominika. Lucas could tell the conversation hadn't been pleasant, but his father seemed determined to see this thing through.

"We're all going," he announced.

Aleksandra said nothing. In the time he'd spent with them, Lucas had never seen them quarrel. Now they were arguing over . . . Kevin Morgan.

"Let's go." His father bent to kiss his wife. She resisted initially, but finally caved in. As they left the apartment, an indignant Coco barked her fury at having to guard the residence. Lucas was on her side, and barely masked his resentment toward the interloper. Outside they waited for a taxi.

"How was your date?" Aleksandra asked, linking her arm with his.

"Terrible. He spiked my drink."

He caught Kevin's loopy smile. "Sounds like a classy guy."

"He was gorgeous. And his wig didn't fit."

Aleksandra looked aghast. "His wig?"

"What about his underpants?" his father asked. The absurdity of the question made Lucas laugh. It must have been infectious. They all laughed, easing the tension between them. By the time they'd arrived at Dominika's upper west side apartment, they were all excited to hear the sonata.

Dominika took one look at Kevin Morgan and instantly forgave them.

"Who is this divine creature? I know I've seen you somewhere before."

"He's a model," Lucas said, not sure why the idea popped into his brain.

"Yes, I model underpants." Kevin grinned when the other three laughed.

"No, you don't. I know who you are." Dominika slapped his arm. "You're that actor . . . why did you say you model underpants?"

"Because for some reason the mention of underpants makes them all laugh. See? Underpants."

Lucas couldn't stop laughing.

"Yeah, I was right about you." Kevin shook his head. "You're a weirdo." As they walked into Dominika's tightly packed salon, he whispered into his ear, "a beautiful weirdo."

ABOUT THE AUTHOR

A. J. Llewellyn divides her time between California and Hawaii. Bags of Kona coffee in the fridge and a healthy collection of Hawaiian records keep her refueled when she is on the mainland. She has written nearly 300 gay erotic romance novels, and she wants you to read them all.

She never lacks inspiration for her male/male erotic romances and has to force her fingers from the computer keyboard to pursue her other passions: collecting books on Hawaiiana, surfing and spending time with family, friends, and her animal companions.

A. J. Llewellyn believes that love is a song best sung out loud. To find out more about A. J., visit her website at http://www.ajllewellyn.com.